RACE WITH
BUFFALO

RACE WITH BUFFALO

AND OTHER NATIVE AMERICAN STORIES FOR YOUNG READERS

COLLECTED AND EDITED BY
RICHARD AND
JUDY DOCKREY YOUNG

August House Publishers, Inc.
LITTLE ROCK

12-94 -BT -19.95

Published by August House, Inc.,
P.O. Box 3223, Little Rock, Arkansas, 72203,
501-372-5450.

Printed in the United States of America

10 9 8 7 6 5 4 3 2 1

LIBRARY OF CONGRESS CATALOGING-IN-PUBLICATION DATA

Race with Buffalo and other Native American stories for young readers /
collected and edited by Richard and Judy Dockrey Young. — 1st ed.
p.   cm.
Includes bibliographical references.
ISBN 0-87483-343-4 (HB): $19.95
ISBN 0-87483-342-6 (PB): $9.95
1. Indians of North America—Folklore. 2. Tales—United States.
I. Young, Richard, 1946– . II. Young, Judy Dockrey, 1949– .
III. Title: Race with Buffalo.
E98.F6R33   1994   94-6145
398.2'08997—dc20   CIP

First Edition, 1994

Executive editor: Liz Parkhurst
Project editor: Rufus Griscom
Design Director: Ted Parkhurst
Cover Design: Wendell E. Hall
Illustrations: Wendell E. Hall

This book is printed on archival-quality paper which meets the
guidelines for performance and durability of the Committee on
Production Guidelines for Book Longevity of the
Council on Library Resources.

AUGUST HOUSE, INC.   PUBLISHERS   LITTLE ROCK

to Chief Jim Fire Eagle
of the Uto-Aztecan Tribe of Kansas

Contents

Preface

The Native American People, whom Columbus mistook for the people of India and miscalled "Indians," discovered, explored, settled, and inhabited the Western Hemisphere over a period of perhaps twenty thousand years, long before the Europeans came to this continent. The Indians respected the earth and used stories to teach their young people that respect. The Native American stories also explained how the world was created, how the animals came to be the way they are today, how the spirits of the dead continue to live in the spirit world and sometimes interact with the world of the living, and how young women and men of Indian tribes could be strong and brave to bring honor to their People.

Some of the stories collected in this book may be so old that they came with those first settlers from Asia two hundred centuries ago. Others were created in more recent times, perhaps even after the European people came to the Western Hemisphere. We have no way of knowing for sure how old these stories are because the Native American tribes did not record history the way we do today (although many tribes had systems of picture writing done on rock, bark, or animal skins).

In the twentieth century, especially in Oklahoma, Native American stories have been shared at a new kind of intertribal ceremonial that has come to be known as the "powwow." We collected these stories by hearing each one of them told twice or more at gatherings, festivals, and powwows. Each of these stories is told by more than one tribe or band of Indians.

Originally the tribes from whom these stories come were scattered across North America, but as the European settlers moved further and further west across the North American continent, they drove the Indians westward ahead of the "white" settlements. Many Indians went of their own free will, in order to get away from the European civilization, which they thought did not respect the earth or the spirits. Other Indians were forced off their tribal lands by greedy white people who wanted the land or the valuable minerals like gold or silver that lay underneath the land. The government of the United States first promised the Eastern Indian tribes western land in exchange for land the whites took away from them, and many tribal groups settled in the Indian Territory now called eastern Oklahoma.

In 1865, one tribe, the Sioux, began a war with the white settlers and soldiers in the Great Plains. Because the white people were afraid that all the Indians might join the Sioux in that war, the Native American People who were living peacefully in many parts of the United States were forced to leave their homes and go to Oklahoma. Only the Indians in the Far West and desert Southwest were left alone on their tribal lands.

By the 1800s, over 60 different tribes comprising most of the Native American population lived in the area that is now the state of Oklahoma. There the Indian way of life was kept alive, the traditions and ceremonies of the tribes honored, and the storytelling traditions preserved.

The editors of this collection are both of Native American ancestry and first heard Indian stories from Oklahoma's rich tribal heritage in their own families. Cynthia McKinney, a Seneca of Sandusky living in northeast Oklahoma in the 1870s, married Benjamin F. Young and was the great-grandmother of Richard Alan Young. Susie Anna Ragsdale, a Chickasaw living in the Chickasaw Nation in 1890, married Laney L. Dockrey and was the grandmother of Judy Dockrey Young.

As storytellers and story collectors, we operate exclusively in the oral tradition: each of the stories in this anthology was first told to us by other storytellers and Native Americans. In each case, we have retold only those stories that we have heard from more than one source, and we have striven to preserve the power and the spirit within each narrative.

We are indebted to the many Native American storytellers who shared their stories with us over the years, who are honored in the Acknowledgments and Notes near the end of this book.

We offer these stories to a new generation of readers, listeners, and future storytellers.

—*Richard and Judy Dockrey Young*
Stoneridge, Missouri

Introduction:
Native American Voices

Well over 12,000 years ago, the first native voices sounded in North America. Since then, this land has reverberated with the voices of Native American orators, storytellers, singers, and shamans. Pride in the ability to speak well has long been a Native American trait, and today it is as alive as it was in the days of Tecumseh, Handsome Lake, Sequoia, and Chief Joseph. It is a cruel irony that, for so many years, the movie and television stereotypes of Indian speech depicted inarticulate grunting and broken language. "Ugh," says the Italian actor hired to portray a plains Indian. "Me have wampum to trade."

In truth, the text of historic Native American stories and speeches show them to have been rich in metaphor, graceful in diction, and strikingly poetic.

THE APPEAL OF MYTHS IN THE MODERN AGE

The traditions of Native American myths, legends, and folktales strike a responsive chord in those who read and hear them today. A growing interest in Native American origin myths is shaped, in some measure, by the historical realities of the age in which we live. Elaine Jahner, in "Lakota Genesis: the Oral Tradition," (1987) suggests that we need cosmological myths all the more now that we live in a scientific era that rejects them. Many people are studying Native American narratives in their attempt to understand fundamental, visceral questions posed by life in the nuclear age. Within the stories they are finding images that teach about life "at the threshold of a new but still endangered world" which surprisingly mirrors the moral dilemmas we face as technology creates new worlds for our society.

THE THRILL OF TALES TWICE TOLD

Age-old Indian tales embraced all of nature, from how a butte or canyon came to be to why fate operates the way it does. There were animal stories much like Aesop's fables that carried lessons in morality and adventure tales about travels to other lands, to subterranean realms and places above the clouds. There were heroes and monsters, riddles and mysteries. Roger Welsch, in "Rising To Speak" (1984), relates that when French trappers and traders visited the plains in the 18th and 19th centuries, they brought along a rich repertoire of European fairy tales and legends. These they traded with the Indians, tale for tale, around many a campfire. Soon Native American storytellers incorporated the exciting elements of European stories into their own tales. There came to be stories of young girls left behind locked doors in lodges, men with seven-league moccasins, and wells full of golden coins—delightful additions to an already richly textured genre!

THE BLESSING OF HUMOR

One trait that has always seen Native Americans through troubled times, and continues to do so today, is humor. Indian stories and ceremonies are filled with clowns. In stories of tricksters, sometimes the trickster is the hero, sometimes the villain; sometimes he is clever, sometimes hopelessly stupid. He is often a very confusing character.

The Navajo call him *Mai*, the coyote; the Sioux, *Iktome*, the spider; the Cherokee, *Tsistu*, Great Rabbit; the Inuit, *Tulugak*, the Raven. His nearest counterparts are Br'er Rabbit (which was adapted from Choctaw tales), Bugs Bunny, and the Roadrunner. Is he a hateful villain or a lovable clown? Is he good or bad? Roger Welsch contends that the trickster is all those things—prankster, wise warrior, eternal vagabond, blind fool. He is what we are. He enacts the human dilemma.

Will Rogers, of Oklahoma Cherokee descent, took his humor to the stage as an entertainer. "My folks didn't come over on the Mayflower," he said, "but they were here to meet the boat." The power and eloquence of the spoken word is not confined to serious Native American oratory in modern times any more than it was in historic times. Today's Indian comment about the landing of Columbus is, "Uh-oh, there goes the neighborhood!" And about the rumored landing of a UFO on Indian land, "Oh, no. Not again!"

THE PASSING OF TALES AT THE POWWOW

Today, as in times past, Native American myths, legends, jokes, and tales, are passed from generation to generation. Rather than around a campfire, today's storytellers may be found in Native American homes, in school classrooms, in urban Indian centers, and at powwows in both rural and urban settings. In addition to the traditional passing of tales from generation to generation, the intertribal powwow has provided a setting for the passing of jokes and stories from tribe to tribe and even to non-Indians.

The powwows that continue today grew out of intertribal gatherings on the plains. Large gatherings of people for ceremonial and celebratory purposes were a common feature of plains history. Communal summer bison hunts brought together linguistic groups, such as the bands of the Cheyenne, for a common purpose. During reservation times, groups of people confined to the reservation, no matter what their tribe or language, gathered together once a year for the disbursement of rations and annuities. The Fourth of July was an especially popular time for these government distributions. Throughout the reservation period, there were also constant visits between reservations for special events such as large dances and give-aways.

By the beginning of the twentieth century, large tribal and intertribal gatherings were often called homecomings, picnics, celebrations, or, after 1925, powwows. The term *powwow* is an Algonquian word. In the seventeenth century, it was listed in Roger Williams's (1827) dictionary of New England Algonquian words, spelled *Pawwaw,* to mean "priest." It also referred to the healing ceremonies held by these priests, who were called "medicine men" by later European settlers. By the nineteenth century *powwow* was used in American English literature to mean a gathering of a number of people in order to make a decision. Oklahoma Indians adopted the term as the name of their intertribal dances in the 1920s.

These dances featured feather and buckskin clad men called "fancy dancers" and women dressed in beautiful appliquéd skirts and shawls. A group of singers sat around a large drum in the middle of a round dance arena and sang the old songs of the plains and woodlands. Shortly after World War II, Native American veterans who settled in cities took the powwow to the urban setting and soon the Oklahoma-style powwow could be found around the nation.

In the 1990s, the powwow has become an amalgamation of many styles of singing, dancing, and regalia from both the Southern and Northern Plains and many other regions of North America. It has transcended the regionalism of pre-World War II America with a national Native American identity. It is not surprising, then, that jokes and stories have moved from one region to another so that storytellers know the oral literature of many tribes. New stories about hard times in the city or on the reservation and about what it means to be a Native American today emerge in the form of stories, jokes, plays, and poems.

Today's eloquent Native American voices continue to be heard, telling of wrongs, past and present, of problems and possible solutions. Most of all, they tell of the traditions of Native American culture and character that remain worthwhile in both the Indian and non-Indian worlds. Roger Welsch believes we haven't "stolen" nearly enough from Native America. "We have left the best treasures unlooted—profound harmony between man and the land, a sense of wonder in the miracles that occur about us on a daily basis, and the understanding of the power of a word well-spoken."

—Gloria A. Young
University Museum
University of Arkansas
Fayetteville, Arkansas

REFERENCES

Jahner, Elaine. 1987. "Lakota Geneses: The Oral Tradition." pp. 45-66 in *Sioux Indian Religion,* Raymond J. DeMallie and Douglas R. Parks, eds. (Norman: University of Oklahoma Press).

Welsch, Roger L. 1984. "Rising to Speak." pp. 112-115 in *Nebraskaland Magazine,* 62 (1).

Williams, Roger. [1643] 1827. "A Key into the Language of America or an Helpe to the Language of the Natives in that Part of America Called New England." pp. 17-163 in *Collections of the Rhode Island Historical Society I.*

Gloria Alese Young is employed by the University of Arkansas, Fayetteville, as the Education Coordinator for The University Museum and an Instructor in the Anthropology Department. She holds a Ph.D. from Indiana University, Bloomington, with a major in Cultural Anthropology and minors in Ethnomusicology and Folklore. Her dissertation, published by the University of Nebraska Press, is an ethnohistory of the music, dance, and traditions which came together to form the Oklahoma-style powwow of this century. She can often be found enjoying the present-day powwows of eastern Oklahoma and western Arkansas.

In Ancient Times

Many Native American stories are set in the days when the world was newly created. These stories were used to show the People their place in the plan the Creator had for the world.

Each of these stories is a part of a much longer story that today would be called an "epic." Each different Indian tribe has an epic story that tells how the world began in ancient times.

The Twin Brothers

*A story of the Caddo People of Arkansas,
Oklahoma, Texas, and Louisiana*

Many, many winters ago, there lived a young man who had learned the secrets of plant and animal lore. He knew which plants and herbs cured illness, which could be used to purify the body and spirit, and which could help the People see more clearly their thoughts and dreams. He came to be known as Medicine Man.

Medicine Man loved a young girl named Clay Pot Woman, and she loved him. She chose him as her husband, and they were married in a ceremony witnessed by their entire village. They built their grass house outside the village, near the river.

One winter later, Clay Pot Woman was going to have a baby. But she grew ill, and the birth of the baby was a difficult time for her. Medicine Man was very afraid for Clay Pot Woman.

Medicine Man went out and gathered all the good herbs and plants to make the strongest medicine he could for both body and spirit. He made a drink from some of the herbs. He burned some of the other plants in the fire to make a good smell and purify the air in the grass house. Other plants he placed at the head of Clay Pot Woman's bedding, to give her spirit comfort and strength.

After a difficult birth, Clay Pot Woman presented Medicine Man with a new baby son. Medicine Man gathered up all the herbs and what was left of the drink, the dirty bedding with all the things left over from the birth and threw them on the midden pile, where garbage and broken pots were thrown. The medicine mixed with the things left over from birth and a magic event occurred: up from the midden pile sprang another baby boy, larger than the one inside the grass house.

Because the medicine was so strong, the second boy born was larger and seemed older already. According to Indian custom, that would make him the older brother. Because he was not born in the grass house, he ran away into the forest and grew up with the wild animals.

Winters came and went, and the young boy born in the hut grew up. Medicine Man and Clay Pot Woman loved him and taught him well. He was known by a boyhood name, but he looked forward to the day when he would be a hunter or warrior and earn himself a manhood name. For that day, Medicine Man made the boy a strong bow and many straight arrows, and the boy spent many happy days practicing his bowmanship.

One day in summer, Medicine Man went out to

hunt and Clay Pot Woman took one of her pots to the nearby river to get water for the day. The boy played in the bare yard that his tribe always cleared around their grass houses.

The boy's mother did not return when the sun was high in the sky; she did not return as the shadows of evening grew long across the grass house; she did not return as the sun went down behind the trees. Medicine Man came home, but not Clay Pot Woman.

Fearing for his wife's safety, Medicine Man took his son with him to the river's edge. There they saw the footprints of Clay Pot Woman; they saw her pot lying broken by the riverbank. Two sets of footprints went into the river. No footprints came back out.

Medicine Man knelt in the clay at the river's edge and wept. "The ogres from across the river have come and taken her away," he said. "The tribe of creatures that lives over there eats people for supper. My wife, your mother, is gone forever." The boy also knelt and wept with his father.

Medicine Man and his son went back to the grass house, built a fire, and stayed inside and mourned for six days. On the seventh, with all their food gone, Medicine Man prepared to go hunting again.

The next morning he said good-bye to the boy and told him to stay near the clearing that was their yard, near the protection of the village. Medicine Man promised to return before sundown.

The boy played in the yard as usual and shot his arrows into a wooden target. Suddenly, when the sun was high in the sky, another boy stepped out of the forest and greeted him. The other boy was taller and

stronger and appeared older than the younger son of
Medicine Man, but he resembled their father, and he
looked very much like the younger boy's reflection in
the water. The Wild Boy had a nose just a little bit too
long, like an animal's snout, and his hair was long and
unkempt. He wore no clothing at all, but he spoke
gently and the two boys played together.

They laughed and joked, and shot the bow in turn,
each trying to better the other's aim. They became fast
friends. At last, the Wild Boy revealed his secret.

"I am your older brother," he said, "born out of
Father's magic. But you must not tell Father about me;
I choose to live in the forest."

As the sun was setting, the Wild Boy left quickly.
Medicine Man came home with game for supper.

For four days it was the same. Each day, Medicine
Man left the grass house to hunt or to go into the
village. The Wild Boy came, and the twin brothers
played together. At sunset, the Wild Boy left, saying,
"You must not tell Father about me; I choose to live
in the forest."

Each night, missing the companionship of his new-
found brother, the younger son moped about the grass
house and stared vacantly into the fire. His father
noticed, and asked what was troubling him. The boy,
who would never lie to his father, told him all about
the Wild Boy.

"We must capture him," said Medicine Man joy-
fully, "and bring him into our house to become part of
our family! When you see him tomorrow, walk to him,
and pretend that you see a little bug crawling in his
long hair. Tell him you will remove the bug, but instead

tie four knots in a hank of his hair. By this magic we will capture him, and bring him into our family. I will transform myself into a flying insect, and hide in the grass nearby."

The next day, Medicine Man became an insect and sat on a blade of grass at the edge of the yard. The Wild Boy came.

"Where is our father?" he asked, suspiciously.

"He is not here," said the younger brother, for in fact, their father was not present in his usual form.

"Then who is that man on that blade of grass?" asked the Wild Boy, and he ran into the forest.

Four more times they tried to fool the Wild Boy. Medicine Man became a bird; he became a dog; he became a crawling bug and hid behind the fire. Every time, the Wild Boy saw him. Finally, the father told the younger boy, "Today I must go hunting. But if your brother should come, try to tie the magic knots anyway."

Medicine Man took his bow and arrows and left the grass house, but a short walk away from the yard he stopped and hung his weapon on a tree limb. He transformed himself into an insect and returned to the yard without his younger son's knowledge.

The Wild Boy came again. "Where is our father?" he asked.

"He is not here," said the Village Boy, unaware of their father's presence.

The Wild Boy smiled, came into the yard, and they played together.

"Brother," said the Village Boy, "you have a bug in your hair. I will take it out." With that, he tied four knots in a hank of the long hair. Just then, Medicine Man became himself again, and he and the Village Boy took the Wild Boy by the arms and led him into the grass house.

Medicine Man took a sharp shell and snipped off the excess nose from the Wild Boy and cut his hair like the boys of the village wore it. He gave the Wild Boy a robe made of buffalo calfskin to wear.

Later, their father gave the boys supper, and while they ate, he went for his bow and arrows. When he returned, to show the Wild Boy that he was welcomed into the family, Medicine Man presented him with a very special arrow, blackened from the smoke of herbs burned in the medicine fire.

To show his love for his younger son as well, Medicine Man gave a blue arrow to the younger boy, painted with juice and oils of many medicinal plants.

The Wild Boy, now dressed and behaving as a proper village brother should, cut bark from an elm tree and made a wheel of bark for the two boys to shoot at. They painted the target in two colors: black and blue. They spent many happy hours in target practice, sometimes rolling the wheel of bark along the ground to test their skill with a moving target.

One day the wheel rolled into the forest without either boy hitting it. When they went to look for it, it was gone.

"Someone has been here, watching us," said the Wild Boy, "and he has taken our target wheel!"

The twin brothers grew stronger and taller as the winters came and went, and the three were very happy as a family. One day in the spring, while their father was away for many days, the Wild Boy said to the Village Boy, "The time has come for us to take our manhood names. Let us go on a long journey."

Each took his own bow, made from the wood of the bois d'arc tree, and his arrows, and parched corn to eat on the journey. The Wild Boy also carried his black arrow, the special gift from their father.

The twin young men walked the path deep into the forest, along the river. The Wild Boy led the way, and they left the path to go into the dense woods. There they met a great squirrel, larger than a dog, who was a friend of the Wild Boy.

The great squirrel gave the twins two pecans that had unusual power within them. The great squirrel told the Wild Boy that his many friends in the forest remembered him and missed him. This gift was a remembrance from the animals and birds in the deep woods.

When night came, the twins made camp and planted one of the pecans in the soft earth. When they awoke the next morning, a great pecan tree had grown overnight. It was so tall that its upper branches were among the clouds, up in the World of Dreams.

The Wild Boy explained to his younger brother: "The Great-Father-Above has special gifts to give us as we reach manhood. He promised me the gift when I was a very little boy living in the forest. Now I will climb high in this tree and see a vision, a dream. All my bones will drop out of my body and fall to the ground. The head bone will fall last of all. You will think that I am long dead, but it will not be so.

"Take my bones and put them in a pile, with the

head bone on top. Cover the pile with my buffalo calf robe and shoot the black arrow into the air. Then, just as we did when we played together and shot our arrows into the air to watch them turn and fall to earth, call out to me, 'Look out, Brother, for the arrow is coming straight toward you!'"

The younger boy was afraid to look up as the Wild Boy climbed, and just as he had said, soon the bones began to fall, the head bone last of all. The Village Boy gathered the bones, covered them, and shot the arrow. He called out, "Look out, Brother, for the arrow is coming straight toward you!"

The Wild Boy ran out from under the calf robe, whole and healthy as ever, just before the arrow struck the buffalo hide.

"Now," said the older boy, "you must also climb up and see your vision, your dream, and receive the powers the Great-Father-Above has reserved for you. I shall do as you did for me, and we will meet here below afterwards."

The Village Boy was fearful as he climbed into the clouds, but soon he felt warm and comfortable, as if he were asleep, and he saw a vision of power. He felt no pain as his bones fell out of the cloud and struck the earth.

But he did hear his brother call out to him, and he ran out from under the buffalo robe, whole and healthy as ever. The arrow struck the hide and trembled, upright.

"What gift did you receive?" asked the older brother.

"Listen," said the younger brother, delighted. And

he opened his mouth and spoke a word that rumbled like an earthquake and echoed off the trees and rocks.

"We will call you by the name Thunder," said the older brother.

"What powers did you receive?" asked Thunder.

"Look," said the older boy, and he opened his mouth and spoke a word that lashed out of his mouth like a snake's tongue, and flashed like flames reaching across the sky.

"We will call you by the name Lightning," said Thunder.

The long day was ending, but strengthened by their new powers and their new manhood names, Lightning and Thunder walked together to the edge of the great river that also ran past their village. As they laid down to sleep for the night, they planted the second pecan.

By daybreak, when they awoke, another great pecan tree had grown overnight. Its long branches drooped across the river, giving them a way to pass over.

Lightning and Thunder climbed up the second great pecan tree and walked down its drooping branches to the opposite side of the river. There, after walking only a short distance, they came to the village of the ogres, creatures that ate people for supper. They saw piles of bones here and there in the grass.

"Look!" cried Lightning, pointing at a pile of bones. "These are the bones of our mother!" How he knew this, Thunder could not imagine, but he trusted his brother's wisdom.

Quickly they piled all the bones in a heap, and the

head bone last of all. They put the buffalo robe over the bones and Lightning shot the black arrow into the air.

"Look out, Mother," called Thunder, "for the arrow is coming toward you!"

The black arrow flew higher and higher in the sky, shot by the greatest strength Lightning could gather; it turned slowly, and fell to earth, faster and faster. Suddenly Clay Pot Woman ran out from under the robe, and the black arrow struck the ground so hard it pierced deep through the calf robe and shattered into splinters.

Despite the many years she had been gone from among the People, Clay Pot Woman knew both her sons the moment she saw them. They embraced and wept with happiness.

Just as they hugged each other, the Great Chief of the Ogres came from the grass house nearby. He was very ugly and very cruel. As he approached, Thunder drew his blue arrow and notched it onto his bowstring.

As the ogre chieftain drew closer, the brothers saw he was wearing their target wheel as an ornament on his right side. By this, they knew he was the ogre that had crossed the river, that had watched them, and that had taken their mother so long before.

Taking aim at the ogre's side, Thunder sent the blue arrow at its target and the great beast-man fell dead.

Before the rest of the ogre village was aroused, the three People ran back to the pecan branch and crossed the river. As they were on the branch, the first of the ogre warriors came running out of the village and came at the People, throwing spears. Thunder turned back and spoke his word, and the great roaring rumble rolled out across the water and frightened the ogres from ever coming across the river again.

Once Thunder had helped their mother down the tree trunk, Lightning turned back and spoke his word. A great white bolt of lightning writhed out of his mouth and split the great pecan tree so that its drooping branches fell into the river and washed away. No People would cross the river to the land of the ogres out of curiosity.

Soon the three People were back at the village, and they came into the grass house and greeted Medicine Man. He embraced them all, and they were a family again.

They lived happily for many years, but finally the day came when Medicine Man, old and having lived a good life, died quietly. Clay Pot Woman did not stay long in this world without her husband; she soon was also dead.

Lightning and Thunder, now grown men, took the bones of their mother and father, wrapped them in buffalo robes, and buried the bundles as their People had always done.

Then, no longer wanting to be in this world, Thunder and Lightning went back down the forest path they had traveled so many years before, climbed the first great pecan tree, and stepped off into the clouds. The old tree fell away beneath them and became a long log in the forest.

Thunder and Lightning lived thereafter in the sky and came and went with the wind and the storms, the

People below looked up and remembered. When they gathered around their fires at night, they told the wonderful story of the Twin Brothers.

Grandmother Spider Steals the Fire

A story of the Choctaw People of Tennessee and Mississippi

The Choctaw People say that when the People first came up out of the ground, People were encased in cocoons, their eyes closed, their limbs folded tightly to their bodies. And this was true of all People: the Bird People, the Animal People, the Insect People, and the Human People.* The Great Spirit took pity on them, and sent down someone to unfold their limbs, dry them off, and open their eyes. But the opened eyes saw nothing, because the world was dark: no sun, no moon, not even any stars. All the People moved around by touch, and if they found something that didn't eat them first, they ate it raw, for they had no fire to cook it.

---

* These terms are explained in the glossary that begins on page 169.

All the People met in a great powwow, with the Animal and Bird People taking the lead, and the Human People hanging back. The Animal and Bird People decided that life was not good, but cold and miserable. A solution must be found! Someone spoke from the dark, "I have heard that the people in the East have fire." This caused a stir of wonder, "What could fire be?" There was a general discussion, and it was decided that if, as rumor had it, fire was warm and gave light, they should have it too. Another voice said, "But the people of the East are too greedy to share with us." So it was decided that the Bird and Animal People should *steal* what they needed: the fire!

But, who should have the honor? Grandmother Spider volunteered: "I can do it! Let me try!" But at the same time, Opossum began to speak. "I, Opossum, am a great chief of the animals. I will go to the East, and since I am a great hunter, I will take the fire and hide it in the bushy hair on my tail." It was well known that Opossum had the furriest tail of all the animals, so he was selected.

When Opossum came to the East, he soon found the beautiful, red fire, jealously guarded by the people of the East. But Opossum got closer and closer until he picked up a small piece of burning wood, and stuck it in the hair of his tail, which promptly began to smoke, then flame. The people of the East said, "Look, that Opossum has stolen our fire!" They took it and put it back where it came from and drove Opossum away. Poor Opossum! Every bit of hair had burned from his tail, and to this day, opossums have no hair at all on their tails.

Once again, the powwow had to find a volunteer chief. Grandmother Spider again said, "Let me go! I can do it!" But this time, a bird was elected—Buzzard. Buzzard was very proud. "I can succeed where Opossum has failed. I will fly to the East on my great wings, then hide the stolen fire in the beautiful long feathers on my head." The birds and animals still did not understand the nature of fire. So Buzzard flew to the East on his powerful wings, swooped past those defending the fire, picked up a small piece of burning ember, and hid it in his head feathers. Buzzard's head began to smoke and flame even faster! The people of the East said, "Look! Buzzard has stolen the fire!" And they took it and put it back where it came from.

Poor Buzzard! His head was now bare of feathers, red and blistered looking. And to this day, buzzards have naked heads that are bright red and blistered.

The powwow now sent Crow to look the situation over, for Crow was very clever. Crow at that time was pure white, and had the sweetest singing voice of all the birds. But he took so long standing over the fire, trying to find the perfect piece to steal that his white feathers were smoked black. And he breathed so much smoke that when he tried to sing, out came a harsh, "Caw! Caw!"

The Council said, "Opossum has failed. Buzzard and Crow have failed. Who shall we send?"

Tiny Grandmother Spider shouted with all her might, "LET ME TRY IT PLEASE!" Though the council members thought Grandmother Spider had little chance of success, it was agreed that she should have her turn. Grandmother Spider looked then like she looks now—she had a small torso suspended by two sets of legs that turned up toward her head and two sets of legs that turned the other way. She walked on all of her wonderful legs toward a stream where she had found clay. With those legs, she made a tiny clay container and a lid that fit perfectly with a tiny notch for air in the corner of the lid. Then she put the container on her back, spun a web all the way to the East, and walked on tip-toe until she came to the fire. She was so small, the people from the East took no notice. She took a tiny piece of fire, put it in the container, and covered it with the lid. Then she walked back on tip-toe along the web until she came to the People. Since they couldn't see any fire, they said, "Grandmother Spider has failed."

"Oh, no," she said, "I have the fire!" She lifted the pot from her back, and the lid from the pot, and the fire flamed up into its friend, the air. All the Bird and Animal People began to decide who would get this wonderful warmth. Bear said, "I'll take it!" but then he burned his paws on it and decided fire was not for animals, for look what happened to Opossum!

The birds wanted no part of it, as Buzzard and Crow were still nursing their wounds. The insects thought it was pretty, but they, too, stayed far away from the fire.

Then a small voice said, "We will take it, if Grandmother Spider will help." The timid humans, whom none of the animals or birds thought much of, were volunteering!

So Grandmother Spider taught the Human People how to feed the fire sticks and wood to keep it from dying, how to keep the fire safe in a circle of stone so it couldn't escape and hurt them or their homes. While she was at it, she taught the humans about pottery made of clay and fire, and about weaving and spinning, at which Grandmother Spider was an expert.

The Choctaw remember. They made a beautiful design to decorate their homes: a picture of Grandmother spider, two sets of legs up, two down, with a fire symbol on her back. This is so their children never forget to honor Grandmother Spider—Firebringer!

OLD MAN AT THE
BEGINNING

Old Man at the Beginning

A story of the Crow People of Montana and Wyoming

A t the beginning of the world, there was nothing but water. It was dark in the world, and no one saw the water of the world. Then the Old Man of the Crow People came into the world, and he looked all around and said, "Is there nothing in this world but water?"

Off in the distance, Old Man saw that there were two little ducks swimming about. These ducks had red eyes. Old Man called them to him. They came swimming, paddling in the world of water.

Old Man said to them, "Is there nothing in this world but water?"

The elder duck answered, "We have never seen anything in this world but water, but we think that there may be something down under the water. We feel it in our hearts."

"Dive down, Younger Duck," said Old Man, and the younger of the little ducks dove deep under the water, looking for the bottom. He was gone a long time, and Old Man said, "Oh, I am afraid Younger Duck has drowned."

"No," said Elder Duck, "we are able to hold our breath for a long time. He will come back up." At about that time, Younger Duck came up with something in his bill. It was a root.

"If there is a root," said Old Man, "then there must be earth as well. Dive down, Elder Duck, and see if you find some earth."

The elder duck dove deep, and was gone for a very long time. When he came up, he had a ball of mud in his bill.

"This is what I have been looking for," said Old Man. He took the root and put it in the ball of wet earth, and blew three times on it. Once he blew, twice he blew, and again he blew on the ball of earth. The ball began to grow and fill the world and push the water aside. It grew until there was a great land, with many plants and animals living on it.

The ducks, who live in water, on land, and in the sky, brought up the earth, and Old Man made the world for the Crow People.

Race with Buffalo

A story of the Cheyenne of the Great Plains

There was a time when all the animals lived in peace, when no one ate anyone else. All the animals were the same color, because they had not yet painted their faces.

Buffalo was the largest and strongest of the animals, and he was getting hungry. He wanted to be the chief of all the animals. He wanted to draw strength from all the other animals by eating their flesh. Buffalo wanted to become the eater of all the animals.

The Human People also said that they should become the chief of all the animals. People wanted to draw strength from all the other animals by eating their flesh. People wanted to become the eaters of all the other animals.

Buffalo challenged the Human People to a race; the winner of the race would become the chief of all the animals. The People said that they would accept such a challenge, but since buffaloes have four legs and People have only two, the People claimed the right to have another animal run the race in the People's place. The buffaloes consented.

The People chose the Bird People to represent them in the race. They chose Hummingbird, Meadowlark, Hawk and Magpie. All the other animals and birds wanted to join in the race, too, each of them thinking that just maybe they too had a chance to become chief of all the animals. All the animals took paint and painted their faces for the race, each according to his or her spiritual vision.

Skunk painted a white stripe on himself as his symbol for the race. Antelope painted himself the color of the earth for the race. Raccoon painted black circles around his eyes and around his tail. Robin painted herself brown with a red breastplate.

The race was to be held at the edge of the Black Hills at the place known as Buffalo Gap. The competitors would race from the starting line sticks to the turn-around stick and then back to the starting line. All the animals, painted according to their visions, lined up between the sticks. Among the animals were the Bird People who would run the race with their wings for the Human People, and Runs-Slender-Buffalo, the fastest runner of all the buffaloes.

The cry was given to begin and all the animals and birds set out on the race. Hummingbird took the lead, ahead of Runs-Slender-Buffalo, but his wings were so small that he soon fell behind. As the animals neared the turn-around stick, Runs-Slender-Buffalo took the lead. Then Meadowlark came up beside Runs-Slender-Buffalo, and the two went along side-by-side right into the turn. Runs-Slender-Buffalo wheeled around the stick, her hooves thundering, and she pulled away from Meadowlark, who went wide to make the turn.

The animals in the lead passed the late-runners who were still headed for the stick. Meadowlark fell behind and cheered on Hawk as he passed her. Hawk gained on Runs-Slender-Buffalo, and it looked like he might pass her. Her heart was pounding and her legs were tiring. But Hawk's wings were tiring also, and he soon fell behind.

Runs-Slender-Buffalo was nearing the finish line as the winner. It looked like the Buffalo People would become the eaters of all the animals!

Then, behind the buffalo woman, wings beating steadily, came Magpie. She was not a quick starter, but her wingbeats were hard and true. Her heart was strong. Her eyes did not wander from the finish line. She never looked back. Her wings were wide and she drove herself forward with beat after beat after beat. All the other animals had fallen behind. Runs-Slender-Buffalo was closing in on the starting sticks, her hooves pounding and dust boiling up behind her. Magpie came slowly alongside. Runs-Slender-Buffalo looked over at the magpie, but the magpie never looked away from the starting sticks.

With each beat of her wings she moved past Runs-Slender-Buffalo by no more than the length of her bill. At the starting sticks, many animals began to line up to watch the finish. Raccoon, who had fallen out of the race early, had returned to the starting sticks. Now he stood up between the sticks and put out his little hands for the runners to touch as they passed. He would feel the touch of whoever was in the lead, and turn toward the winner.

Closer and closer came Runs-Slender-Buffalo, and some of the animals feared Raccoon would be trampled. Magpie gradually flew nearer to the ground so she could brush Raccoon's little hand as she flew past. Raccoon did not move, but stared straight at the onrushing pair. Magpie seemed to be pulling ahead. Runs-Slender-Buffalo leaned forward as she ran to touch Raccoon's hand with her great nose.

Magpie's wingtip touched Raccoon's little hand and he turned toward her an instant before Runs-Slender-Buffalo thundered past and he was surrounded by a great cloud of dust. All the animals waited breathlessly for the dust to settle. At last, there stood Raccoon with his little hand raised toward the path of Magpie.

The Human People had won the race!

The buffalo wandered the great plains and ate grass, and the People became the great hunters, the chief of all the animals.

Blue Corn Maiden
and the Coming of Winter

A story of the People of the Eight Northern Pueblos along the Rio Grande in New Mexico

Blue Corn Maiden was the prettiest of the corn maiden sisters. The Pueblo People loved her very much, and loved the delicious blue corn that she gave them all year long. Not only was Blue Corn Maiden beautiful, but she also had a kind and gentle spirit. She brought peace and happiness to the People of the Pueblos.

One cold winter day, Blue Corn Maiden went out to gather firewood. This was something she would not normally do. While she was out of her adobe house, she saw Winter Katsina. Winter Katsina is the spirit who brings the winter to the earth. He wore his blue-and-white mask and blew cold wind with his breath. But when Winter Katsina saw Blue Corn Maiden, he loved her at once.

He invited her to come to his house, and she had

to go with him. Inside his house, he blocked the windows with ice and the doorway with snow and made Blue Corn Maiden his prisoner. Although Winter Katsina was very kind to Blue Corn Maiden and loved her very much, she was sad living with him. She wanted to go back to her own house and make the blue corn grow for the People of the Pueblos.

Winter Katsina went out one day to do his duties, and blow cold wind upon the earth and scatter snow over the mesas and valleys. While he was gone, Blue Corn Maiden pushed the snow away from the doorway, and went out of the house to look for the plants and foods she loved to find in summer. Under all the ice and snow, all she found was four blades of yucca.

She took the yucca back to Winter Katsina's house and started a fire. Winter Katsina would not allow her to start a fire when he was in the house.

When the fire was started, the snow in the doorway fell away and in walked Summer Katsina. Summer Katsina carried in one hand fresh corn and in the other many blades of yucca. He came toward his friend Blue Corn Maiden.

Just then, Winter Katsina stormed through the doorway followed by a roar of winter wind. Winter Katsina carried an icicle in his right hand, which he held like a flint knife, and a ball of ice in his left hand, which he wielded like a hand-ax. It looked like Winter Katsina intended to fight with Summer Katsina.

As Winter Katsina blew a blast of cold air, Summer Katsina blew a warm breeze. When Winter Katsina raised his icicle-knife, Summer Katsina raised his bundle of yucca leaves, and they caught fire. The fire melted the icicle.

Winter Katsina saw that he needed to make peace with Summer Katsina, not war. The two sat and talked.

They agreed that Blue Corn Maiden would live among the People of the Pueblos and give them her blue corn for half of the year, in the time of Summer Katsina. The other half of the year, Blue Corn Maiden would live with Winter Katsina and the People would have no corn.

Blue Corn Maiden went away with Summer Katsina, and he was kind to her. She became the sign of springtime, eagerly awaited by the People.

Sometimes, when spring has come already, Winter Katsina will blow cold wind suddenly, or scatter snow when it is not the snow time. He does this just to show how displeased he is to have to give up Blue Corn Maiden for half of the year.

Bears' Lodge

A story told by the Kiowa People in Wyoming and South Dakota, and by other tribes

One day long ago a traveling party of the Kiowa People were crossing the great prairie and camped by a stream. Many of the Bear People lived nearby, and they smelled the Kiowa People. The Bear People were hungry, and some of the bear warriors went out to hunt the Kiowa People.

Seven young girls from the Kiowa camp were out gathering berries, up along the stream, far from the campsite. The Bears came upon them and growled to attack. The girls ran and ran, out across the open prairie, until they came to a large gray rock. They climbed onto the rock, but the bears began to climb the rock also.

The girls began to sing a prayer to the rock, asking it to protect them from the Bear People. No one had ever honored the rock before, and the rock agreed to help them. The rock, who had laid quietly for centuries, began to stand up and reach to the sky. The girls rose higher and higher as the rock stood up. The bear warriors began to sing to the bear gods, and the bears grew taller as the rock rose up.

The bears tried and tried to climb the rock as it grew steeper and higher, but their huge claws only split the rock face into thousands of strips as the rock grew up out of their reach. Pieces of rock were scraped and cut away by the thousands and fell in piles at the foot of the rock. The rock was cut and scarred on all of its sides as the bears fought to climb it.

At last, the bears gave up the hunt, and turned to go back to their own houses. They slowly returned to their original sizes. As the huge bears came back across the prairie, slowly becoming smaller, the Kiowas saw them and broke camp. They fled in fear, and looking back at the towering mountain of rock, they guessed that it must be the lodge of these giant bears. "*Tso' Ai'*," some People say today, or "Bears' Lodge."

The Kiowa girls were afraid, high up on the rock, and they saw their People break camp and leave them there, thinking the girls had all already been eaten by the bears.

The girls sang again, this time to the stars. The stars were happy to hear their song, and the stars came down and took the seven girls into the sky. Like sisters they sit together in the night sky, the Seven Sisters, and each night they pass over Bears' Lodge and smile in gratitude to the rock spirit.

Young Heroes

Girls and boys your age had to learn quickly and work hard in Native American families and villages. They became young adults at a very young age by European standards, and they often had great adventures that called for wisdom, courage and cleverness. These stories about young heroes were told to children to teach them the correct path to follow in personal life, family life, and in the life of the clan or tribe.

The Evening Star

A story of the Caddo of Arkansas, Oklahoma, Texas, and Louisiana

In the ancient times there were many more kinds of Human People and Animal People than there are now.* There were monsters, too. One of the most feared monsters was the water panther. The water panther was a huge horned creature with a head like a cat and fins like a fish. The water panther lived in lakes or streams, and only came up to the surface to feed at sunset. He always came up to eat just as the sun was going down, but he sank back beneath the dark water when the Evening Star appeared.

The water panther's favorite food was the Caddo People, and they were careful not to be in or on the water in a canoe when the sun was just setting.

Once there was a family traveling by canoe down the long rivers of the Southeast. They were from a

---

* These terms are explained in the glossary that begins on page 167.

different tribe and did not know about the water panther. Just as the sun was setting, the head of the great water panther rose above the surface of the river. His head was as big as a grass house of the Caddo People. He came up behind the canoe and opened his great mouth. He ate the man and the woman in the canoe, then sank back beneath the waves before the Evening Star appeared. The canoe drifted to shore just beside a Caddo settlement.

The People came out of their grass houses and saw the canoe on the shore, and went down to it. They knew at once what had happened, for there was blood on the ribs of the canoe.

Just then, they heard a sound. A baby boy was wrapped in a buffalo blanket in the back of the canoe. He had been asleep but was now awake and crying. The water panther had not eaten the baby!

The baby's long hair was tied in a strange way, so the Caddo People knew he was from another tribe. They took him in and raised him as one of their own children. The boy lived twelve springs with the People of that settlement and learned their ways and the ways of the water panther.

One year a drought came upon the land, and all the plants and animals began to suffer. Crops would not grow, even when river water was taken in gourds and poured into the gardens. The river water became dark and foul and muddy, and the level of the river went down. Everyone was hungry. Especially the water panther.

Then some of the People began to talk among themselves and complain about how little food there was. They became angry that the boy from the canoe was living among them. He wasn't one of the People. He was just another mouth to feed!

One of the elders of the settlement called the men together and they made a plan. The next day everyone went in their canoes out in the river to a long narrow island with trees growing on it. They all went hunting among the trees for birds' nests, and they gathered eggs. They built a fire on the sandy shore of the island and had a great feast of birds' eggs. Then everyone lay down to take a nap. The boy lay down, too, and fell asleep.

When the boy awoke, everyone else had gone. Only pretending to sleep, they had left in their canoes while the boy was napping. He was marooned on the island, left there to take care of himself or die. Perhaps the water panther would eat him, this long-overdue meal from the past.

The boy could see the grass houses in the distance, downriver on the far shore. But he knew it would do no good to call for help. He knew he had not been left behind by accident.

The boy searched the island and found more bird eggs, and ate well that night. Just at sunset, the great water panther came up from the riverbed. Its horns were as thick as tree trunks and as long as spears. Its eyes were as big as leather shields used on the warpath. It stared at the boy on the island without blinking.

"Why are you here alone, human boy?" said the water panther in a deep, growling voice.

"I was left behind on this island when the People came to gather eggs," said the boy, telling half the truth.

"I will help you," said the water panther. "Do climb upon my neck. Do hold fast to my horns. I will carry you to the shore." All the while the water panther was thinking, "If I eat this boy, it will be just a small meal. But if I befriend this boy, and the People come to trust me, I will eat well for many nights before they learn my true nature."

The marooned boy climbed onto the water panther's neck, and held its horns, one with each hand. The great creature turned and began to swim slowly across the muddy river.

"You must tell me," said the creature, "if you see the Evening Star appear."

They were halfway across the river, nearing the settlement, when the boy saw the Evening Star. He told the creature, and it turned back and swam to the island. It set the boy off on the sand and sank beneath the muddy waters.

The next day, the boy was hungry. There were no more bird eggs. He could not catch any birds. There were no berries or roots to eat. The water panther was also hungry.

As the marooned boy sat on the shore, staring across the dark water at the distant settlement, the sun began to set. The great head of the water panther broke the surface of the river.

"I will help you," said the water panther. "Do climb upon my neck. Do hold fast to my horns. I will carry you to the distant shore." Again the marooned boy climbed onto the water panther's neck and held onto its horns. The great creature turned and began to swim slowly across the muddy river. "You must tell me," said the creature, "if you see the Evening Star appear."

They were two-thirds of the way across the river, nearing the settlement, when the boy saw the Evening Star. He told the monster, and it turned back and swam to the island again. It barely let the boy off before it sank under the muddy waters.

The next day the boy was very hungry. He had eaten nothing for two days. He wondered if he could swim to the shore. Always in the past the People had not swum in the river because of the water panther. Now the panther seemed to want to help. Might the boy swim across? No, he thought, better not to risk it. There may be another water panther under there who is not so helpful. And what good would it do to get across the river if the People of the settlement would not feed him? At least he would be on good dry land; in the forest he might do better than on this small sand island. He tried to fish, but caught nothing. The water panther must have eaten everything in the river. Finally, the boy sat on the bank as the sun went down.

The dark waters roiled and the two horns appeared, then the great round eyes, then the nose and the mouth with its huge long fangs. The water panther stared at the boy and licked its chops.

"I will help you," said the water panther. "Do climb upon my neck. Do hold fast to my horns. I will carry you to the shore." Again the marooned boy climbed onto the water panther's huge neck and held onto its horns as it turned and began to swim across the river. The boy bowed his head in sorrow and closed his eyes. "You must tell me," said the creature, "if you see the Evening Star appear."

They swam and swam, getting closer and closer to the distant settlement. The sky grew darker and the Evening Star appeared behind them. "Do you see the Evening Star?" asked the water panther.

The boy had been raised to never lie to an elder; it made him sad to betray his upbringing. But his eyes were closed, and he spoke the truth when he said, "No, I do not see the Evening Star."

The creature swam on and was just reaching the shore when the boy opened his eyes and looked behind them.

The Evening Star was coming toward them, coming down out of the sky. It drew closer and closer, and the boy saw that it was a young and handsome man dressed in white buckskin. He carried a bow with many shining arrows, made from the light of the stars. The Evening Star was gliding down like a hawk, coming in for the kill. He had his arms stretched out, then he brought them down and notched an arrow into his bow. The boy thought the Evening Star was about to shoot at him for lying to an elder. The boy rolled off the water panther and hit the wet beach. As the water panther turned, the Evening Star let fly an arrow of starlight.

The arrow struck the water panther and it gave out a huge roar. The arrow went deep into the creature, and a bright beam of burning light shone out of the hole the arrow had left. The creature rolled over and sank beneath the water, which began to boil.

The Evening Star came down and touched one foot

to the earth, and seemed to grow as heavy as a man when he touched down. He walked to the marooned boy and laid one hand on the boy's shoulder.

"Do not be afraid," he said to the boy. "I am the Evening Star. I have tried for many a year to kill the water panther, which was the last of its kind. It killed and ate many animals and People, and only by your help tonight was I able to kill it. Let us go now unto your People and tell them that you are a hero."

"They are not my People," said the boy. "They made me an outcast on that island. I will have to go away from here anyway, so we do not need to tell them anything."

"Then," said the Evening Star, "come and live with me in the sky. You will be my arrow-bringer and we will hunt across the sky for all time."

The Evening Star took the boy's hand and raised his other hand to the sky. As if he were lifted by some giant hand, the Evening Star rose upward. The boy felt himself become without weight, and he floated upward with the Evening Star. The Evening Star shot an arrow into the settlement below, and the arrow told the People the story of the marooned boy.

If you look to the Evening Star today, you will often see a small companion, his arrow-bringer. They hunt across the night sky for all time.

The Flying Head

A story of the Seneca and Seneca of Sandusky People of the Northeast and Midwest, also told in tribes of the Southwest

Long ago there was a great beast called the Flying Head. It was a giant head, as big as a house, with huge wings instead of ears. Its eyes were as big as clay bowls, and its mouth was like a basket full of sharp knives. Its nose was very small, though, and it didn't smell things well. When it got hungry, the Flying Head flew into a village and picked up People and animals and ate them. The Flying Head came in bright sunlight only, and many People simply stayed in their lodges when the sun was bright.

There was a young mother whose husband had been eaten by the Flying Head. She and her baby lived in fear of ever going out in the daylight. Finally one day she decided that it was not right for this Flying Head to come and eat the People and animals of her village. She thought of a plan.

She took her baby to a neighbor woman and left

her for safekeeping. The neighbor woman was always very alert, and would hide with the baby under the house if the Flying Head came. Then the young mother went to a neighbor man and asked him for an armload of firewood. He gave it to her and she went and lit a fire as if she were going to bake bread.

She went to the riverbed and got small round stones just about the size of loaves of fresh bread. She got out her biggest wooden spoon. She got a basket and filled it with sand.

She put the stones in the fire to heat up red hot. She put a bread bowl beside the fire. She put the basket of sand beside the table. She waited for high noon to come.

When the sun was high, she lifted the red hot stones out of the fire with the spoon and set them in the bread bowl. The bowl smoked a little, but it just looked like the bread was steaming. She heard outside the sound of People yelling and running to hide. Someone had seen the Flying Head coming!

The young mother sat at her table, with the bowl of red hot rocks in front of her, and the spoon in her hand, and the basket of sand beside her. She waited, singing loudly as if she were working and alone, unafraid of anything.

Outside she heard the loud whoosh of the wings of the Flying Head. She heard the sound of its awful teeth grinding as it thought about lunch. She sang even louder and more happily, and she lifted a red-hot rock in her wooden spoon.

The Flying Head heard the young mother singing, and, seeing no one else in the village, it flew down to her lodge. The Flying Head hovered outside the window and looked in, first with one huge eye, then with the other.

The young mother lifted the red-hot rock toward her mouth. She opened wide and brought the spoon close. Then she dropped the rock past her face and into the basket of sand. She chewed and chewed as if she had eaten something. Then she rubbed her tummy and said:

"Bread. Good, hot bread."

The Flying Head moved around and stuck its little nose in the window and tried to smell the bread. It sniffed and sniffed but couldn't smell any bread. But its nose was so small that it didn't think anything about not smelling anything.

The young mother picked up another red-hot rock in her spoon, and brought it close to her mouth. She opened wide, but dropped the rock into the basket of sand. She chewed and chewed, and patted her tummy.

"Bread. Good, hot bread."

The Flying Head was getting really hungry for lunch. Even though it usually ate People and animals, the idea of some good hot bread pleased it. The Flying Head stuck its ugly mouth up to the window and said:

"Brrrreeeaaad ... guuuud ... haaaaht ... brrrreeeeaaad ..."

The Flying Head didn't talk very clearly, because of all those teeth in its mouth.

Then it flew to one side and looked in again, first with one eye and then with the other. The young mother went on pretending to eat bread. She didn't offer the Flying Head any bread.

The Flying Head took the roof in its teeth, and tore the roof off the house. It reached its wings in and broke the walls of the house back so it could get its big, ugly self inside. The young mother ran back out of the way.

The Flying Head lifted the bowl of red-hot rocks with its wings, tilted backwards, and dumped all the hot rocks into its mouth. The rocks began to burn and burn and burn and burn.

The Flying Head let out a yell and flew way up in the sky. He spun around and spun around, and exploded into a thousand pieces.

The young mother went and got her baby back. The men of the village fixed her roof and leaned the walls of her house back in place. She made a new bread bowl to replace the one that was all black and charred.

After that day, she and her baby went out and sat in the warm sun whenever they wanted to.

Skunnee Wundee and the Stone Giant

A story of the Seneca and Seneca of Sandusky People of the Northeast and Midwest

Long ago there lived huge men made of stone. They were as tall as a tree and they left deep footprints as big as a cradle-board in the dirt everywhere they walked. Those stone giants never made war against the Human People, and they were very forgetful, being made of stone. They loved to eat Human People, but they forgot this taste for People any time that there weren't any around. The stone giants usually stayed in one place, because they forgot that there was anyplace else to go.

One day a young boy named Skunnee Wundee was out hunting with his bow and arrow, and he wandered up to the river where the stone giants lived. He recognized the river, and knew that if he went too far north along that river, he might be seen by the giants. He knew that if they saw him they would kill him, but he thought he could hunt along the river just a little ways, and turn back before he reached the land of the stone giants. As he walked along the river, he became more and more interested in seeing deer or other animals that came to the river to drink. As he hunted, walking northward, he wandered too close to the giants' home.

As he crept about among the huge rocks along the riverbank where the rapids began, he sat down to rest on the nearest jagged boulder. Suddenly, the rough chunks of stone began to move. They closed over him like fingers and he began to rise into the air. He knew what had happened: he had sat on a stone giant's hand! He quickly threw his bow and arrow away, so the giant would not think he had come to make war.

Slowly the stone hand rose up and turned. Skunnee Wundee was looking straight into the face of a stone giant. Its head was as big as a house, and its mouth was like a canoe full of sharp flint rocks. Its eyes were as big as baskets, but they were cloudy and dull, not sharp and bright like an Indian child's eyes. The giant spoke in a dull, deep voice like rocks grinding together in a rock slide.

"You're a People! I remember about your kind! I eat Peoples!"

Slowly the huge mouth opened, and the sharp, shiny teeth spread apart to crush and tear Skunnee Wundee to bits.

"Wait!" yelled Skunnee Wundee, "I came here to play with you!"

The giant's hand stopped moving.

"Play?" he said slowly, trying to remember what

that was.

"Yes, play! See, I have no bow and arrows, no baskets, nothing. I came empty-handed. Why else would I come here, except to play?" said Skunnee Wundee.

Slowly the giant put the boy back on the riverbank.

"What shall we play?" asked the stone giant, sounding a tiny bit more interested than before.

The only game Skunnee Wundee could think of that a stone giant might like was rock skipping. "Let's skip some rocks," said the boy. He began to look along the bank for a good, flat skipping rock. The giant looked for a big rock for himself.

Suddenly Skunnee Wundee heard a tiny voice calling to him. "Pick me up, Skunnee Wundee! Pick me up, Skunnee Wundee!"

Skunnee Wundee looked down and saw a little green river turtle. He picked it up, and the turtle said in a tiny voice, "Throw me into the river instead of a rock!"

"I've got my rock," called Skunnee Wundee to the stone giant.

"I've got mine," said the giant, lifting a stone as big as a man's body. "I'll throw first." The giant slowly lifted the stone and swung its huge arm. The stone sailed out over the river and hit the water. It skipped four times before it sank.

"Four times," said the stone giant, "Beat that!"

Skunnee Wundee whispered, "Thank you!" to the little turtle, and then he swung his arm and tossed the turtle out onto the river. The turtle pulled its head and legs in, and looked just like a rock as it hit the water.

The turtle's flat bottom hit the water, and it skipped one, two, three, four times. Then the turtle put out its feet and began to kick hard. The kicking turtle looked just like a skipping rock.

"Five!" yelled Skunnee Wundee, "Six! Seven!"

Now the turtle settled into the water, but he began to swim! It looked like the little "rock" was still skipping.

"Eight!" called the human boy, "Nine! Ten!"

The turtle reached the far bank and sat still on the bank with its head and legs pulled in.

"All the way to the other side," said Skunnee Wundee, "I win!"

The stone giant got mad. He threw a temper tantrum. He shook and shook until the stones of his body began to shake loose. Skunnee Wundee ran away and picked up his bow and arrow. As he ran southward, he heard a huge rock slide behind him. He looked back and saw that the stone giant had crumbled into a thousand rock pieces. There was nothing left of him but a huge pile of stones.

The Turkey Girl

*A story of the People of the Eight Northern Pueblos
along the Rio Grande in New Mexico*

They were living at White House Pueblo. There was
a young girl there; she was an orphan and lived
with her relatives. They dressed in fine clothes and
went off to a dance at Pecos Pueblo, leaving the Turkey
Girl, as they called the orphan, to feed the flock of
turkeys. Turkey girl was dirty and dressed in rags. Her
hair was thick with grime and full of lice because she
was made to work all the time and never had the chance
to bathe or make any clothing for herself. As she was
feeding the turkeys, the oldest turkey spoke to her!

"Why have you not gone to the dance at Pecos
Pueblo?" he asked.

She told him she had nothing to wear, and she was
dirty. He called all the turkeys together. They helped
the girl wash her hair with yucca soap, and the turkeys
picked the lice from her hair. Then each turkey presented itself to the girl and asked to be hit with the stick
used to stir the fire.

When she hit the first turkey, fine beaded moccasins fell out of his feathers. When she hit the second turkey, out fell a white dress. From another fell a black shawl. From another fell beads, from another fell a belt, and so on until she was dressed as nicely as anyone. The oldest turkey used his beak to tie her hair in very pretty knots on the sides. Then she was ready to go.

She thanked the turkeys, put out food and water for them, and she left to go to Pecos Pueblo.

On the way, a handsome warrior saw her walking along the road. He fell in love with her and ran to his house, where he lived with Gah-mah-ku Baba, the Spider Grandmother. He asked Spider Grandmother for a kicking-stick toy made of fine turquoise and she gave him one. He went down the road kicking it. He kicked it right in front of Turkey Girl. She bent down and picked it up. She smiled and handed it back to him. They walked together and became friends. Soon they arrived at Pecos Pueblo.

At the dance young men came from all over to give Turkey Girl gifts, trying to win her favors. No one knew who she was—even the people who raised her did not recognize her. She danced almost all night and then went home with Spider Grandmother's grandson. She slept at Spider Grandmother's house until morning.

When the sun came up, Spider Grandmother's grandson proposed marriage to Turkey Girl, but she turned him down. She walked back to White House Pueblo to take care of her beloved turkeys.

When she got home, her family was there. Only

then did they recognize her. She told them of how the turkeys had helped her, but her mean family would not believe her. Instead they accused her of being a witch!

Turkey Girl and her friends the turkeys left the house that day to go out and search for food, as they did every day. But this day they went to the south instead and went to the Shipap, the hole in the earth that goes to the spirit world.

Turkey Girl and her friends the turkeys went back into the earth and into the spirit world, and they were happy, far away from the cares of this world.

Magical Beasts

Indian children love stories about monsters, just as all children do, and when stories are told around the fire, scary stories are often requested.

Although many Native American stories describe creatures and monsters that we have never seen today, these two stories are about beasts with more magic than most.

Long Hair and Flint Bird

A story of the Ácoma Pueblo of west central New Mexico

L ong ago there lived an Ácoma man named Long Hair. He was a brave warrior and a great hunter. Ever since his wife died, Long Hair had been both father and mother to his young son. In those days the Ácoma People lived in fear of the Flint Bird, a great flying monster whose feathers were sharp flint arrowheads and whose favorite food was the Ácoma People. If a man was alone on a high place, or a child played too near the edge of the mesa, Flint Bird might swoop out of the sky and eat them. Long Hair made his son promise never to go out alone or wander far from the house.

One day, while the boy was playing near the house, and Long Hair was inside making bread for them to eat, Flint Bird came and took the boy up into the air. Long Hair ran out with his bow and arrows but could not hit Flint Bird.

Long Hair laid prayer sticks and rubbed herbs on

his body to give him strength. He went down off the Ácoma mesa and walked to the foot of the mountain where Flint Bird lived. The Ácoma People watched him sadly, as he sang his song and climbed down. No one had ever returned from Flint Bird's nest.

After many long days' journey, Long Hair rested under a tree and sang the Ácoma war song. Spider Woman was spinning a web in the tree above and she greeted Long Hair. He told her of his journey to try to rescue his son, and she invited him into her underground house for the night. She came down on a string of web and opened the trap door into her house under the ground. Long Hair became very small through the magic of Spider Woman, and they went into the house together. The house was beautiful. On the walls were white doeskin clothing and beautiful weaving. Necklaces of turquoise hung on pegs on the walls. Spider Woman's daughters were busy on their looms weaving pretty blankets of red and white and brown. Spider Boy, their brother, came home from hunting, but he was embarrassed that what he had brought would fill his family, but not Long Hair—even a small Long Hair.

Long Hair took his corn meal out of his travel pouch to share. He ate very little, no more than the spiders ate, so as not to seem to be a glutton. The next day, like a good guest, Long Hair did not rush out to go to the mountain of Flint Bird. He stayed and went hunting with Spider Boy, and they became good friends. Long Hair pulled out some of his own hairs and made snares to catch birds. They caught many snowbirds and ate a feast that day. Long Hair helped dry the meat for the house. He wove tiny mattresses of snowbird feathers for the two daughters' beds. He helped Spider Boy with his chores. He was a perfect guest. Spider Woman told her son Spider Boy that Long Hair was the finest man she had ever met, and that the spider family should help him in his long journey to rescue his son. Spider Boy agreed.

Spider Woman sent Spider Boy on a fine strand of web up to the house of Flint Bird. Spider Boy chewed herbs and blew into the house. The magic of the herb breath put Flint Bird to sleep. Spider Boy examined the flint cape that Flint Bird wore when he flew. Then Spider Boy came back down the strand of web to the house in the ground.

The next day Spider Woman took what she had learned from her son, and helped Long Hair make a cape of wings. The feathers were made of pine chips dipped in boiling pitch. They stuck together and shone just like flint. When Long Hair wore the cape, he too could fly.

Outside the spider house, Long Hair was his full size. Spider Boy was tiny, and rode holding Long Hair's long hair. Long Hair put on his pine-and-pitch wings and they flew up to the mountainside to Flint Bird's house. Outside, Spider Boy again chewed herbs and blew into the house. While Flint Bird slept, Long Hair traded wings with him.

Then Long Hair flew up above the house on the flint wings and made loud noises. Flint Bird jumped awake and put on the pine-and-pitch wings, thinking they were his. Outside, Long Hair declared that he had come for his son. Flint Bird refused, and the fight began! Flint Bird called on his friends the icy winds, and he covered the mountain top with snow. The wind blew Long Hair to the mountaintop, where Spider Boy spun a web over them both to keep them warm. When the snow melted, Long Hair rose up again to fight. Flint Bird was amazed. He thought this rival birdman had been frozen to death!

Flint Bird began to bargain with Long Hair.

"I will return your son unharmed if you can prove you are more worthy than I am."

"What must I do?" asked Long Hair.

"Pull all the weeds from my cornfield before sunset!" said Flint Bird. The field was huge and there were thousands of weeds. Long Hair began to work.

"Keep working," said Spider Boy, "I will be back shortly." After the sun was growing low, and only a part of the weeds were pulled, Spider Boy came back and handed Long Hair a web end. Just as Flint Bird came out to laugh at Long Hair's failure, Spider Boy said, "Pull the web." Long Hair pulled and the web, which ran to every weed in the field, pulled all the weeds up at once with one mighty tug by Long Hair. Flint Bird saw all the remaining weeds jump from the ground at once, and his laughter turned to anger.

"Now you must pick all the corn and gather wood to roast the corn in my great oven! You must do this before darkness comes and the stars come out!" said Flint Bird, and he went back into his house.

Spider Boy called his friends the badgers, and told them to dig a secret room beneath Flint Bird's great oven. He called his friends the packrats and told them to bring all the wood they could find. Then he spun a web over all the ears of corn while Long Hair started the fire in the oven. The packrats left a huge pile of wood and ran quickly away so that Flint Bird would never know. The badgers dug the secret room under the oven and crept away in silence. Spider Boy gave Long Hair the web end, and he pulled all the corn off the stalks and into the oven with one mighty tug.

Flint Bird came out and found the corn roasting in the full oven. The stars were coming out. Long Hair sat by the oven awaiting the cruel bird. Flint Bird laughed, and shoved Long Hair, with Spider Boy on his shoulder, into the hot oven. Flint Bird slammed a rock over the opening. Long Hair and Spider Boy crawled into the warm secret room the badgers had dug, and there they spent a pleasant night.

The next day Flint Bird came out to eat his cooked rival, but he could not find Long Hair in among the hot roasted corn. Long Hair came out of the secret room, and out the oven door unharmed. Flint Bird was furious!

"Sit beside me on the fire!" shouted Flint Bird. "We shall see who is the mightiest!"

Flint Bird took his shovel and pulled the corn out of the oven. He took some of the leftover wood and built a new fire in the oven. Flint Bird, wearing the pine-and-pitch wings that he thought were his, climbed into the flames. He pulled Long Hair in beside him and Long Hair sat in the flames in the flint cape he had stolen.

Each birdman began to chant a death chant. Flint Bird chanted a cruel threat. Long Hair chanted the war chant of the Ácoma. Each birdman began to dance the war dance in the flames. The flint cape kept Long Hair from burning, at least for a while.

But Flint Bird's pine-and-pitch wings smoked and curled and burst into flame. Flint Bird screamed and was burned up. Long Hair ran out of the oven and threw off the red hot flint cape.

Long Hair took Spider Boy off a tree onto his shoulder, and they went into Flint Bird's house and found a room full of captives in clay jars. They set Long Hair's son and the captives free and took all Flint Bird's soft buckskins, bead necklaces, bows, arrows, and weavings and gave them to the captives. Long Hair kept one beautiful doeskin robe for Spider Woman.

The Ácoma People walked down the mountain and visited Spider Woman's house. Long Hair introduced her to his son, and told her and Spider Boy that they would always be welcome in the houses at Ácoma. Then they journeyed home, climbing the mesa to their village, and had a great feast.

The Bloodsucker

A story of the People of the Eight Northern Pueblos along the Rio Grande in New Mexico

When evening fell on the upper Rio Grande River, there used to be a terrible spirit that floated up and down the steep-walled river valley. If anyone was out walking along the riverbank right at sunset, this evil spirit would fly down and suck the blood right out of them. They would fall down dead and dried up like a withered squash.

One day a young woman gave birth to her first child. It was a pretty girl. The woman and her husband lived in an adobe brick house outside the pueblo of Okeh-Oyngeh. The man had built the house high above the river to keep it from getting washed away when the river flooded. The house was quite a long walk from the pueblo.

After the birth, the young mother stayed at home four days for a cleansing ceremony. But the young father was eager to take the baby across the river to his pueblo, the village of Yunkeh-Yunkeh, so his mother could see her new granddaughter.

The next day, the man was doing his chores and gathering firewood. According to custom, the young mother's sisters should come and be with her during this time. The sisters were supposed to name the baby. The man wanted to go into the pueblos and tell the sisters that the baby had been born.

After four days, the man, the woman and the baby went down to the pueblo for a ceremony. After the ceremony, the young man's mother, who was very superstitious, encouraged them to return home with the child immediately. The grandmother believed the baby should not spend the night away from her home until she was given her name. The grandmother urged them to leave quickly since it was almost twilight.

The young couple said good-bye and left in a hurry. It looked like they would have plenty of time to get back to their house before the sun began to set and the evil spirit came out. But they journeyed homeward too slowly. They were just crossing a log footbridge over the Rio Grande when the sun touched the horizon and the spirit came out of a cave at the base of the steep walls of the high riverbank.

The Bloodsucker rushed like a wind down the river valley and sucked all the blood out of the mother and child. The young man, who was walking just ahead of them to protect them, was left unharmed. The spirit swept on up the river looking for other victims. The young husband ran to his house and prayed to the good spirits. He was filled with anger and grief.

He asked the good spirits to give him courage and strength. He put sacred corn meal on his face. He prayed and sang. Then he knew what to do.

The next day, he spent all day cutting fresh young trees to get wood to make spears. He made the spears straight and sharp. Then he gathered the spears and set out in early afternoon to go down to the river. He found a trail of blood on the tips of the grasses. This trail led to the Bloodsucker's cave. He followed the blood and found the cave. He stuck all the spears into the soft earth all around the cave mouth. He fixed them with all their sharp points inward, making a ring of death.

As the sun was about to set, the young man stood outside the cave and sang an angry song, calling the Bloodsucker out. The sun touched the horizon and the Bloodsucker raced out of his cave. He was angry for the things the young man had sung about him. He rushed out like the wind to kill the young man.

As the Bloodsucker hit the ring of sharp spears, they cut him into thousands of tiny pieces and killed him.

The blood trail on the grass turned into the plant with beautiful red flowers now called the Indian Paint-brush.

The thousands of pieces of the Bloodsucker turned into mosquitoes.

So now if you go down to the Rio Grande near the ancient abandoned pueblos of Okeh-Oyngeh and Yunkeh-Yunkeh, there are mosquitoes there.

And they will suck the blood right out of you.

Laughing Stories

Before the European and African people came to the New World, the Native American People did not tell jokes the same way we all do today. Instead of jokes, the Indians told laughing stories. Native American stories always have more than one purpose; very seldom is a story told just to make the listeners laugh. While these tales also have lessons and morals, they are more laughable than most.

Bear's Race with Turtle

*A story of the Seneca, other Northeastern tribes, and
the Seneca of Sandusky of the Midwest*

One fine snowy day, Bear was walking through the
snow in the forest. When he walked up on a little
hill and stood up on his hind legs, he was so much taller
than anything else he could see that he was very proud.
Bear loved to brag about how splendid he was, so he
thumped himself on the chest and roared, "I'M THE
BIGGEST ANIMAL IN THE FOREST!" And nobody
made a sound, because Bear really was awfully big.

Bear got an itchy spot on his back, so he walked
through the snow to a little tree, leaned against it and
wriggled around. While he was scratching, the whole
tree broke with a snap! Bear was so impressed with
how strong he was, once more he roared out, "I'M THE
STRONGEST ANIMAL IN THE FOREST!" And nobody
said anything, because Bear really was very strong.

Bear began to run down off that little hill. Now,
every human child learns very early that you can run
like the wind downhill. But Bear was so impressed

with how fast he could run, he skidded to a halt by a little frozen lake and roared, "I'M THE FASTEST ANIMAL IN THE FOREST!"

Then Bear heard a little voice pipe up from the edge of the lake, "No, you're not, Bear! I'm a lot faster than you!"

"WHAT?!" Bear couldn't believe his ears. Then he couldn't believe his eyes! Because that voice came from a little green water turtle, who was sticking his head up through a hole in the ice.

Turtle said it again. "Really, Bear, I'm a lot faster than you are." Bear and Turtle began to disagree, then to argue, and then they began to make so much noise that the other animals came to see what was going on. A great argument was in the making when it was decided that the only way to settle the question was to have a race between Bear and Turtle. The animals reached a general agreement: the race would be around the lake. But then Turtle said, "I'm a water animal, so I'll have to race in the lake."

Bear objected, "You must think I'm pretty stupid! You can just dive under the ice, then come back up and say you won!" Though the animals did think he was pretty stupid, he had a point. So a solution was agreed upon. Bear, who was a land animal, would race around the lake, while Turtle would swim from one hole in the ice to another, put his head up and say something, then swim on. Fox, who had no reason to cheat in this case, was chosen to be the starter and judge, and the race was scheduled for the next day.

The next morning, Elk, who had the biggest feet, was chosen to punch holes in the ice every few feet. All the animals had heard about the race and had come to see it. Almost all the spectators were making bets, and because most of them were so tired of listening to Bear brag, the bets were heavily in favor of Turtle.

Fox called the racers to his side. "Are you ready, Bear?" Now Bear had been warming up, doing exercises, and getting in some last minute bragging, so he yawned and said, "Yeah, I'm ready." Fox asked, "Are you ready, Turtle?" And Turtle, at his first hole in the ice said, "I'm ready!"

"Alright," said Fox, "Once around the lake and back to me. Now ... RUN!"

Turtle dived under the water, and Bear began to just walk, waving casually to his friends, just to prove how easy this was going to be. But Bear had only taken a couple of steps when Turtle's head came up in the second hole in the ice.

Turtle said, "Come on Bear, catch up with me!" And Turtle dived under and went on. Bear was flabbergasted! This turtle was faster than he thought, so Bear began to jog a little faster. But only three steps farther, Turtle's head popped up at the next hole. He said, "Come on, Bear, catch up with me!" then dived under and went on.

Now, Bear knew he had to run! He dropped to all fours and began to run as fast as he could. But before Bear passed the third hole, Turtle came up at the fourth hole and said, "Come on, Bear, I'm way ahead of you!"

Bear ran and ran as fast as he could, his tongue drooping further and further out of his mouth, so out of breath he thought he would drop. But, that turtle just kept getting farther and farther ahead, each time popping out of a hole to say, "Come on, Bear, catch up with me!" Until finally, when Bear was only half way around the lake, Turtle finished the race!

A great cheer went up from the other animals, "TURTLE IS THE FASTEST ANIMAL IN THE FOREST!" Even those that hadn't bet on Turtle came down to congratulate him and shake his clawed foot and pat his shell.

And Bear? Well, Bear was exhausted, and so humiliated that he didn't even finish the race. He turned and went to his house, which was a cave, and slept the rest of the winter. And to this day, bears sleep all winter so they don't have to remember losing that race to a turtle!

There was a big party and feast in Turtle's honor, and then, finally, everybody went home.

Now, Turtle looked around carefully, making sure everyone was gone. Then he crawled down to the edge of the ice, stuck out his clawed foot and rapped three times on the ice.

Suddenly, up through the holes in the ice came Turtle's brothers and sisters, his mom and dad, his aunts, uncles, cousins near and distant, even his grandma and grandpa turtles were there, and everyone of them looked exactly like Turtle! They nodded their heads at each other and said, "Yes, we are the fastest animals in the forest!"

Turtle said, "Thank you, my kinfolks. Today we have proved that though we turtles may be slow of foot, we are not slow of *wit!*"

Cricket and Cougar

A story of many tribes of Alta and Baja California

Cougar was walking in the forest, and he jumped onto a fallen log to look around. From inside the log came a tiny voice.

"Get off the roof of my lodge!" Out from the rotten end of the log came tiny Cricket. "You are standing on the roof of my lodge, Cougar," said the little insect. "You must step off now, or the roof-pole will break and my lodge will fall in."

"Who are you to tell me what to do?" asked Cougar sternly, although he did step off the log. He lowered his head until his nose was very close to Cricket. "In this forest, I am the chief of the animals!"

"Chief or no chief," said Cricket bravely, "I have a cousin who is mightier than you, and he would avenge me."

"I don't believe you, little insect," snarled Cougar.

"Believe me or believe me not," said Cricket, "it is so."

"Let your cousin come to this place tomorrow,

when the sun is high, and we will see who is the mightier," said Cougar. "If your cousin does not prove himself to me, I will crush you and your entire lodge with my paw!" Cougar turned and bounded off through the forest.

The next day, when the sun was high, Cougar came back along the same trail. He stepped over the log and called out to the cricket. "Cricket, come out! Let me meet your mighty cousin!"

Just then, a tiny mosquito flew up from the log and buzzed into the big cat's ear.

"What's this?" cried the cougar, who had never seen or heard a mosquito before. The mosquito began to bite the soft inner ear of the cougar, and drank from his blood. "Ahrr! Ahrr!" cried the cougar in pain, "Get out of my ear!" The cougar pawed at his ear, and ran around in a circle shaking his head. The mosquito bit him again and again.

Cricket came out of the log and called up to the cougar. "Are you ready to leave my lodge alone?"

Cougar said that he would so Mosquito came out of Cougar's ear and went into the log lodge with Cricket. Cougar ran off down the trail, and never went that way again.

The Two Sisters' Husband

A story from the Caddo of Arkansas, Oklahoma, Texas, and Louisiana

There were two sisters living with their parents in one village of the Caddo People. They were both very pretty, and many men wanted to marry them. After a while they began to enjoy the favors of their suitors so much that they started to think of themselves as being too good for the men in their village.

"I don't like Buffalo Man," one sister would say. "He smells bad."

"I don't like Rat's Brother," the other would say. "He has funny teeth."

Fairly soon they had eliminated as possible husbands every young man in the village. Then they decided to go to a neighboring village to pick husbands. They announced to their parents that they were going away to marry.

They went down the path, further than they had ever gone before. They walked all day and thought that by now they must be coming to another village.

Suddenly, they met a man on a crosspath, carrying a turkey. He looked surprised to see them. His hair was tied in a funny way, and he spoke a little differently than the girls did, so they knew he was not from their village.

"I make you welcome in my village," said the man. "I am U'ush," he said, which means owl. The sisters greeted him and introduced themselves. They told Owl that they had come from far away seeking husbands. Wanting only the best husband for themselves, they asked, "Is the chief of your village married?"

Owl said, "No, he ... I mean, no, I am not. I am the chief, and I am not married. Why don't both of you girls come to my house and be my wives?" According to Caddo custom, women could choose their husbands, and neither men nor women were limited to only one spouse.

The sisters liked the idea of both being wives of a chief, so they agreed. Besides, Owl was fairly good-looking, and they had already turned down everyone in their own village.

"Let me run ahead and tell my grandmother that you are coming to be my wives," said Owl. "You wait here." And he ran off down the path carrying the turkey. The sisters thought it was strange that a chief should have to run ahead, but this was not their village; perhaps the ways of the villagers here were strange.

"Grandmother," called Owl as he ran into his grass house, "there are two foolish sisters from a nearby village who have come looking for husbands. They think I am the chief! You must help me fool them into marrying me." Owl's old grandmother laughed a toothless laugh. Owl said, "When we come in you must greet me as if I were chief. And when you ask what I want for supper, I will tell you I want turkey. Then, you say that you will go to our vast herd of hundreds of turkeys and kill one." The grandmother laughed again as Owl ran back out the door, still carrying the turkey. Owl ran back to where the sisters were waiting up the path. He greeted the girls again and led them to his house at the edge of the village. The girls thought it was strange that a chief should live at the edge of the village instead of at its center, but this was a strange village, and perhaps their ways were strange as well.

As they entered the house the grandmother called out, "Oh, great chief, my grandson. Welcome to your house. What would you have for dinner with your new wives?"

Owl answered, "Tonight I think I should like … turkey!"

"Oh, great chief, my grandson," said the old woman, "I will go and kill one of our vast flock of turkeys …"

"Wait, Grandmother," said Owl, holding up the turkey he had been carrying all this time, "We will eat this one instead."

After supper, Owl told his new wives that it was time for sleep. "It is a heavy burden that I bear in council house," he said, "and I must get some rest." The girls were tired from their long walk, and they slept well under warm buffalo robes. The next day Owl was up early and told the sisters that he had to go to the council house on village business, and that they should just make themselves comfortable and do no work all day.

"Let us walk you to the council house," said the sisters.

"It is forbidden for you to go into the council house," said Owl, "but you may walk me part way." They went with Owl to a place near the center of the village, where the council house sat, and they saw Owl go in and heard the singing just after he entered.

"It is good to be wives of the chief," they said.

That evening, Owl returned late, carrying a turkey.

"Oh, great chief, my grandson," said the old woman, "welcome to your house. What would you have for supper this evening?"

"This evening," said Owl, "I think I would like a turkey."

"Oh, great chief, my grandson," said the old grandmother, "I will go to our vast herd of turkeys and kill ..."

"Wait," said Owl, holding up the turkey he was carrying, "let's eat this one."

After turkey stew that night, the sisters wanted to talk, but Owl was tired and his back hurt. "It is a heavy burden that I bear in council house," he said. Owl went on to bed, and the girls sat and amused themselves watching the stars.

The next morning Owl was up early, but the sisters were troubled. Where was Owl's cape of feathers? Where was his mace? He didn't seem to dress much like a chief. Owl told the sisters to stay at the grass house all day, and not to wander about the village. "It isn't proper for a chief's wives to wander about."

The sisters had a plan: they announced that they were chief's wives, and would stay in bed and sleep late any day they wished. And today they so wished. They pretended to turn over and go back to sleep.

The grandmother was glad to hear this; she was tired of waiting on these girls hand and foot. She eagerly left the house and went to laugh with her friends about the two foolish sisters.

The sisters saw the grandmother and Owl go off in opposite directions, and they quickly got up and followed Owl without him seeing them.

He went straight to the center of the village. The sisters followed, hiding behind trees and houses as they went. Owl went right into the council house. The sisters ran over to the cane screen that kept anyone from looking directly into the council house. They looked around the screen.

There was Owl, walking to the empty space at the head of the circle of men! Owl got to the chief's space, and began to sit down. The men of the council began to sing. It was true Owl *was* the ...

But then, out from behind another cane screen came the real chief, wearing a feather cape and carrying a stone mace. Owl got down on all fours, and the fat chief sat down on Owl's back, so he could be higher than all the others seated at council. For this task, Owl was paid the handsome sum of ... one turkey a day.

"Owl!" screamed the sisters, "You fooled us! You are not the chief! You are the chief's *chair!*"

At that, Owl jumped up, dumping the chief in the dust. He ran after the sisters who ran down the path toward their own village. He tried to get them to come back, but they didn't stop. They ran all the way home.

That year each sister took one of the village boys as her husband, and each lived happily in their own grass house in their own village, where they never had to worry about strange ways again.

How and Why Stories

Young People ask so many questions that sometimes the elders turn to stories to explain "how and why" the world got to be the way it is today.

Some of these "how and why" stories are small bits of longer epic stories about the ancient times. The epics were only told aloud at special occasions, but these shorter stories could be told to children at any time or place.

The Ballgame Between the Animals and the Birds

A story of the Cherokee People of Oklahoma, North Carolina, and Georgia

Once the Animal People challenged the Bird People to a ballgame.* The animals expected to win with no problems.

Bear was the captain of the animals' team. "Of course we'll win," roared Bear. "I'm stronger and heavier than any other animal." It was agreed that Bear could stop anyone that got in his way. And Deer? Deer could outrun all the other animals. And Terrapin was at that time the great, original terrapin, not the puny thing we have now. So of course the animals would beat those silly birds!

The Birds had, of course, elected Eagle as their captain. They also had the skills of the great, mythical

---

* These terms are explained in the glossary that begins on page 169.

Hawk. The birds had met to plan their strategy—they were a little afraid of all the animals, who were so large and strong. But, when the meeting was ready to begin, along came two tiny things that looked a little like field mice.

"Please," said the little creatures, "can we join your team?"

"You belong with the animals, don't you?" said Eagle.

"They laughed at us and drove us away," said the smaller, furry creature. "We want to be birds. Let us help you." Eagle felt so sorry for them that he agreed to let them play as birds.

"You need wings. We'll make you some," said Eagle. The birds decided to use the head of the drum that they used for their dances. The drumhead was made of badger skin, so they began to cut off pieces of it and attach it to the smaller creature's front legs. This is the way the birds created Bat.

Unfortunately, this used all of the drumhead leather. There was none left to make wings for the creature that looked like a tiny ground squirrel.

"Let's stretch the skin he has," said Bluebird. This sounded like a good plan, so Eagle and Red-tailed Hawk pulled from opposite sides, helped by the smaller birds. When they were done, the birds had created Flying Squirrel.

Flying Squirrel and Bat were very grateful. "You'll see! We can help you win."

The animals and birds met on the plain by the river. The ballgame would be won by whoever first hit the ball against the poles at opposite ends of the playing field that were the goals of the birds and the beasts.

The great ballgame was very close. The animals were shocked to see what strong fliers Bat and Flying Squirrel were. The small animals who were too young to play stood at the side of the ball field and began to chant, "Beasts over Birds! Beasts over Birds!"

The hummingbirds began to lead their own chant, "Birds over Beasts! Birds over Beasts!"

Finally, Flying Squirrel caught the ball, carried it up a tree, and then threw it to Blue Jay who flew with it high enough that the animals couldn't reach it. Then Blue Jay dropped it, and Bear rushed to try to take it away. But Bat swooped very near the ground, took the ball, and dodged and doubled so fast that even Deer couldn't catch him. He threw the ball against the pole decorated with feathers and won the game for the birds.

Where the Dog
Ran Across the Sky

A story of the Cherokee People of Oklahoma, North Carolina, and Georgia

The Cherokee People lived in houses of woven sapling branches covered with mud plaster that were gathered in villages. Each house had a corn crib on its side where corn was kept to dry in the air, out of reach of hungry animals. Corn was placed on stone beating bowls and was beaten with wooden posts until it was ground into meal. The meal was made into corn cakes and cornmeal mush and other good things to eat.

Sometimes some of the People would beat more cornmeal than was needed that day, and the meal was put in baskets until the following day. It happened one year that someone was stealing the meal from the baskets at night.

Every morning, the baskets were overturned, all the meal was gone, and there were huge paw prints in the dirt around the houses. The prints were those of a huge dog taller than a man, and larger than a buffalo from the grasslands. The men stood for a long time, looking at the tracks. A giant dog is a dangerous thing.

The head man, the chieftain of the tribe, spoke at last.

"We must not try to hunt this Great Dog. We must not try to kill this Great Dog. Let us hide tonight behind the tall stone bowls we use to beat corn into meal. Let us bring drums and rattles and all kinds of noise makers. When the Great Dog comes to steal the white cornmeal, we will make a great noise and frighten him away."

So that was how it was done. The men hid around the village behind their meal beaters with drums and rattles and all kinds of noise makers. They waited. When the moon rose, a great dog came out of the sky in the west and came toward the rising moon. The Great Dog came into the village as quietly as fog. His fur shone in the moonlight like white fog.

The Great Dog was as tall as a house, and he silently turned over a basket of white cornmeal and ate it in huge swallows. He had white meal on his mouth now. At first the head man was afraid to give the sign for the men of the village to make noise. He was afraid the Great Dog might eat the men instead of the meal. Then, the head man gave the sign.

All the men of the village began to beat the drums and rattle the turtle-shell rattles and shout out loud. The Great Dog was startled by the thunderous sound. He looked up from the basket he had overturned, with his great mouth full of white meal. He turned, ran a circle around the village, and then he ran across the sky to get away from the noise. As the Great Dog ran across the sky, the white cornmeal fell from his mouth and off his muzzle. The white cornmeal scattered in a trail across the sky.

The bright, white trail of stars across the heavens today is called by some the Milky Way, but to the Cherokee People it is known as "Where the Dog Ran Across the Sky."

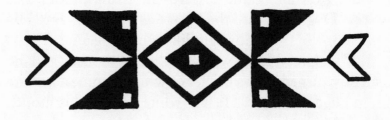

How Bear Lost His Tail

A story of the Seneca and Seneca of Sandusky People of the Northeast and the Midwest

Once Bear had a long, shiny, black tail. The fur of his tail was sleek and black and long and beautiful. Bear liked to swish his tail back and forth for the other animals to admire. One day Bear was walking through the forest in winter time. He came to a frozen lake.

Out on the ice of the lake, Fox was about to eat three fish that he had stolen by running off Otter, who had actually caught the fish. Bear saw Fox and the fish, and lumbered out on the ice to talk to Fox. The ice creaked and groaned under Bear's weight, but it did not crack or give way. Fox saw Bear coming, and quickly thought up an explanation to give to Bear about where the fish had come from.

"Fox," called Bear, "are you having fish for supper? May I join you?"

"Oh, hello, Bear," said Fox. "These little fish? Why you may eat them, Bear. I was just pulling them out of the way so I could catch some really big fish to eat."

"How do you catch the fish?" asked Bear.

"Oh, it's easy," said Fox. "You just dip your long tail down in the water through this hole in the ice, and you twitch your tail to attract the fish's attention. When a really big fish comes over to nibble the fur on your tail to see if it's good to eat, you just stand up and that pulls the fish right out onto the ice for your supper. You have such a long, beautiful tail, Bear. You'd probably catch a lot more fish than I could."

"Move over," said Bear bossily. "I'll catch my own fish now that I know the secret." Bear sat down on the ice and dangled his long black tail into the freezing cold water.

"Oh, there's a big one now," said Fox. Bear turned to look in the icy water to see the fish he might catch. "No, don't turn around! See? You scared him off. Just sit still here, and twitch your tail every once in a while."

Fox picked up the three fish in his teeth and trotted off across the ice to his warm den for supper with his wife and pups.

The next morning, Fox was out wandering the forest, over new-fallen snow, and he decided to go back by the lake. Out on the lake was a huge pile of snow. Fox trotted out to investigate.

The snow mound was snoring quietly.

It was Bear! He had sat there all night, waiting for fish. Now his long tail was frozen in the solid ice, where the fishing hole had closed during the night.

"Hello, Bear!" said Fox brightly.

Bear was so startled that he jumped up. When he jumped up he broke his frozen tail off in the ice! His beautiful tail was gone; all he had was just a short little furry stump of a tail. He was so angry that he chased Fox across the lake and around the forest three times before he went to take a nap.

And to this day foxes and bears don't get along together. Not since Bear lost his tail.

Coyote's Sad Song to the Moon

A story of the People of the Eight Northern Pueblos along the Rio Grande in New Mexico

L ong ago, when the world was young, the sky was very dark at night. The Creator Spirit that had made the world had made the sun to ride across the sky by day, but the night sky was empty. The Creator Spirit heard the prayers of the People and the animals who wanted to be able to see at night. He called on Coyote to come to him and serve him.

Coyote came and waited respectfully, looking down as the Creator Spirit gave him a deerskin pouch tied with a piece of sinew. The Creator Spirit told Coyote to walk a certain path and to open the bag when he came to the highest point on the trail. Coyote was not to open the bag any sooner than the highest point. The Creator Spirit told Coyote that the trail would be long, and he would go many days and nights without rest. He told Coyote to be strong.

Coyote took the pouch and went on the path he had been given.

Coyote was not highly regarded by the People and other animals, and he was proud to have been chosen to take the pouch to the highest point on the trail. At first he walked proudly, the pouch hanging from his mouth, along the path he had been given. As the day wore into night, and the night became day again, Coyote walked less proudly. He grew tired and hungry, and cared less about the great honor that had been given to him. As another night came and went, the spit from Coyote's mouth soaked into the dried deer sinew, and it began to soften, and tasted liked meat.

Before he knew what he was doing, Coyote was chewing on the sinew, just as a hunter on a long hunt will chew on dried meat. Soon the sinew was chewed in two, and the pouch fell out of Coyote's mouth. Coyote was only half-way up the great mountain when the pouch fell. The pouch hit the ground and came open.

Out of the pouch flew thousands of pieces of shiny mica; they flew like the butterflies up into the sky and settled against the blanket of night to become the stars. Out of the pouch rolled a ball of mica, and it rolled up the trail and into the sky to become the moon.

But Coyote was not at the highest point of the trail when the pouch came open, and the moon did not climb into the sky on its proper path. Instead of riding only across the night sky, the moon sometimes comes up at night, and sometimes comes up by day. And it turns this way and that, like a hunter who is lost, looking for the proper path to follow.

Because he did not live up to the trust the Creator Spirit had placed in him, Coyote hung his head in shame. Then he looked up to the moon and sang sadly his apology to the moon for his lack of courage.

To this day, Coyote is He-who-hangs-his-head, and he only lifts his head when he sees the moon. He lifts his head and sings his sad song of apology to the moon for not carrying the pouch to the highest point of the trail.

Kanati the Hunter and the Cave of Animals

A story of the Cherokee People of North Carolina, Georgia and Oklahoma

In ancient times, there was only one Cherokee village. The most prominent family in this village was that of Kanati the Hunter and his wife Selu Cornwoman. Selu first gave the Cherokee People the gift of corn, which is their principal crop. Kanati did all the hunting for the entire village in those days. They had two sons, one born to Selu and another who grew from a clot of deer blood.

It happened like this: one day Kanati brought home a deer to skin and cook, and Selu, who was about to give birth to their first child, took the deer to the creek and washed the blood out of the meat. From a clot of that deer blood grew a wild boy, who was "born" out of the creek at the same time Selu gave birth to her son.

Wild Boy and Younger Brother grew up quickly,

and while Younger Brother was strong and brave, Wild Boy had magical powers. When Kanati came home one day with a deer to butcher, the twin brothers decided to go and find out where their father found so much wild game to hunt. Wild Boy wanted to know where he had come from—he wanted to know about his deer blood ancestors.

Every day the boys tried to follow their father, but every time he saw them. On the first day, he saw Younger Brother and told the boys to go home. On the second day, Wild Boy followed alone, but Kanati saw him and sent him home. On the third day, Wild Boy disguised himself as a bird, but Kanati saw through the disguise and told him to go home. On the fourth day, Wild boy turned into a fluff of down from a bird feather and floated down to land on Kanati's shoulder. In that form he rode along without his father knowing.

Kanati went up to the sacred mountains and followed a trail to a cave blocked by a stone. He pulled the stone aside, and out ran a deer. He put the stone back, hunted the deer, shot it with his arrow, and went home carrying the deer on his shoulders. Wild Boy saw it all and ran home to tell Younger Brother.

The next day, when Kanati had others things to do and was not going hunting, the two boys went along the path to the cave. They listened at the crack around the stone over the cave mouth. They could hear every kind of growl and grunt and bark inside. They could hear the sounds of all the animals there are. The two boys decided to move the stone aside and let out one animal to hunt. They pushed and pulled and grunted and groaned, and they finally moved the rock aside.

Out of the cave ran deer after deer, and as the boys tried to push the rock back over the cave mouth, other animals came out. Bears came out. Panthers came out. Rabbits came out. Badgers came out. Wolves came out. Raccoons came out. As the boys struggled to close the cave off, all the animals that there are came out with the mice last of all.

At home Kanati, who had been the keeper of the animals in the cave, heard the sound like thunder of all the animals running out of the cave, their paws and hooves and feet pounding the earth as they ran. Kanati got up and ran up along the trail to the cave mouth. There stood Wild Boy and Younger Brother beside the opening. They hung their heads in shame.

Kanati said nothing to them at first. He went inside the cave and kicked over the baskets and clay pots full of insects. The bees and wasps and fleas and ants poured out and swarmed on the boys, stinging and biting them.

When the insects had gone their way, free as birds, Kanati spoke to his sons.

"Never before has our life been harsh. When we needed meat, I came to this cave and got meat for us to eat. Now all the animals are as free as birds, and we will have to hunt for the rest of our lives. With our spears, our blow guns and our bows and arrows we will work hard all our lives. We will have to wander the forest hunting. Some days we will come up empty handed. Some nights we will go hungry. All because you were careless and thoughtless. You must always be careful when you are dealing with nature. You must always think before you act in the forest of nature."

And so it is that hunting has been hard work and a labor of great skill among the Cherokee ever since.

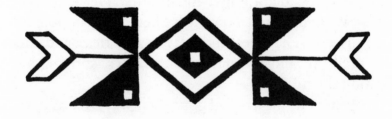

How Buzzard
Got His Clothing

A story of the Six Nations (or Iroquois Confederation) and the Seneca of New England and Oklahoma

When the Creator first made the world, he gave the animals their fur and hair, the fish and snakes their scales, and the insects their shells and wings. But he forgot to give the birds any clothing. The birds had no feathers yet, and could not fly. They were cold. They walked everywhere they went. And all they could eat was dead fish that washed up along the shore. The birds were very unhappy.

The birds met in council and said, "Surely this is not right. Everyone has clothes but birds."

Eagle was the chief of the birds, and he said, "Let us wait until the sun is coming up, and we will all pray. Each bird will sing his song to He-who-holds-up-the-sky."

The next morning, at the crack of dawn, the birds

all began to pray. Woodpecker and Indian Hen played the drum. All the birds sang. Crow cawed and Robin chirped. Lark and Bluebird trilled their songs. They all sang their songs except Mockingbird, who sang little pieces of everyone else's song. Even today, birds sing at dawn.

The prayers drifted up to heaven, and the Creator sent down his helper to the eagle with a message. The helper came to the council fire of the birds and said, "The Creator has heard your prayers and will answer them. Select one among you who will serve as the messenger-to-the-gods, and he will be taken up to the heavens. He will not even need to speak his wishes— the Creator already knows them."

When the Creator's helper had gone back to the sky world, the birds began to discuss who among them should be chosen as the messenger-to-the-gods. Eagle said, "I would go, but the journey may be long, and I have other responsibilities here."

Hummingbird said, "I would go, but I am so small the Creator might not even see me."

Robin was well respected at council, and he said, "Let us send Buzzard. He is both noble and patient." Everyone agreed, and they turned to Buzzard and gave him their blessing. All the birds came up and congratulated Buzzard, who was so proud that he blushed. Robin came up and congratulated Buzzard, and he blushed again, because buzzard was somewhat shy and did not speak to the other birds very often.

Buzzard puffed up his chest and walked proudly out of the council house, and the Creator gave him the power of fight, the first of the birds to have it. As

Buzzard flew higher, he saw the earth shrinking below. Finally, Buzzard reached the sky world. He stepped onto a cloud.

By now Buzzard was swelling with pride; he had lost his humility, which had been his best trait until then. Buzzard was led into the Lodge of the Creator. He stood there for a few minutes, surrounded by clouds, when he heard a voice.

"Buzzard, turn around." Buzzard turned around, and where there had been nothing before, now there were hundreds of beautiful suits of feathers hanging from pegs on the vast walls of the lodge, each different from the next. "Here are the suits of feathers I have made for the Bird People. As their messenger, you have the honor of selecting for your own the suit you like the best. Those you do not choose will fall to earth and become the clothing of the other birds. Take as long as you like to make your selection, but beware: once you have taken a suit of clothing off, you can never put it on again. Choose wisely!"

Then there was silence, and Buzzard began to try on suits of feathers to find one that he liked the best. He tried on the first suit; the wings were brown with little white streaks, and the breastplate was the color of the sunrise—a bold red-orange. Buzzard said, "This suit of feathers is very beautiful, but as messenger-to-the-gods, I need something more colorful." He took off that suit and let it fall. The suit passed through the cloud-floor of the lodge and drifted down to earth. Robin caught it and put it on.

Buzzard took another suit of feathers off its wooden peg and pulled it on. It was bright crimson, with a beautiful black dance mask and crimson mess cap. "This is all one color," said Buzzard and he took it off and let it fall. Cardinal ran and caught the suit and wore it.

Buzzard tried on a gold and black suit, but he didn't like the colors, and let it fall. Finch wears it today.

One suit was brilliant moss green on the wings and back, with a blood-red gorget at the throat. But the suit was a little bit tight, so he let it fall. Hummingbird is wearing it today.

Suit after suit fell from the lodge of He-who-holds-up-the sky, and birds sang their thanks to the Creator and their praise to Buzzard for sending down such beautiful suits for them to wear. Finally Buzzard put on a suit that was brown-black and dull; the suit was too small, and his bare neck stuck out. The wings were wide, but drab and not colorful at all. The leggings didn't reach his feet, so his legs were bare, and there was no cap to wear with his suit, so his head was bare. "I don't like this at all," he said, and he looked over at the wall of the lodge. All the pegs were empty. This was the last suit of feathers! And it was not beautiful at all, in fact it was rather ugly. Buzzard realized how vain he had been, wanting the very best suit for himself. He was so embarrassed at his vanity that he blushed and his head turned red forever.

Buzzard was so ashamed that he flew off alone and ate the carcasses of dead animals rather than go back to the feast at the council house of the birds, where everyone was happy with their feather suits.

The Seven Star Brothers

A story from the Seneca People of the Northeast and Midwest

There were seven brothers long ago who trained to become warriors of the Seneca People. Their uncle sat with them outside their mother's lodge and played on his drum so that they might dance the war dance and learn the warrior's ways. Each day they danced, and their mother became displeased.

When their uncle declared the young men ready, they spoke among themselves and decided to go out along the warpath, because there was, in those days, a war between the Seneca and their neighbors. The seven sons gathered at the war post and began to dance around it, according to the custom, and at the end of the dance they went to their mother and asked for the dried meat and parched corn they would eat on their journey.

Their mother did not want them to go away, since some or all of them might not return from the warpath, and she refused to give them the food they needed.

Three times the seven brothers did the war dance around the war post; three times their mother refused to give them even a single cake of cornmeal bread.

The brothers went again to the war post and this fourth time, the eldest brother changed the song they sang. He sang a magic song, and as he lifted his leg to step a dance step, he stepped up into the air. Each brother followed, and they were soon dancing just above the ground. On the second turn around the war post, the eldest brother again stepped up, and with each round the seven warriors went higher and higher into the air.

Since their mother would not let the eldest son lead his brothers along the warpath, he led them upwards into the sky. Their mother heard the strange song, and the shouts of the People of the village who saw her seven sons climbing slowly into the heavens. The mother ran out of her lodge and called to the eldest son, asking him not to leave her alone. The eldest son's heart was touched, but he did not look down.

The mother called out again, and the eldest warrior looked down. He stumbled in the dance and almost fell from the sky. He warned the other brothers not to look down until they reached the sky world.

Their mother called out a third time, and the sons danced on.

When the mother began to weep and called out to her firstborn son with her arms outstretched, the eldest brother's heart was touched again. He looked down at his mother, stumbled, and fell out of the dance. As the six younger warriors went up into the sky world, the seventh fell to the earth like a falling star and struck the ground near his mother.

The mother ran to the crack in the ground that the falling brother had made. The crack was deep and there was nothing inside it. She looked up and saw that her remaining sons had become a circle of stars, dancing forever around a war post in the sky.

She stayed at the crack in the ground and built her lodge there with her own hands. A green tree grew out of the crack and grew tall like her firstborn son had been. When a hunter slashed the tree to see if its sap was sweet like the maple, blood ran out instead.

The mother bound up the tree's wound and stayed by it. She sang to the tree each night, as she had sung to her firstborn son when he was a baby on the cradle board. In the spring of the year, the tree grew feather bundles like the feather bundles on her son's dance costume. But these feather bundles were made of wood and were the seeds of a new race of trees whom the Seneca named the pine. The children of the pine, when slashed, give sap that the People use in making canoes and ropes. The feather-bundles are the cones of the pine tree today.

When the tree's mother grew old and died, the first pine tree also died, and the spirit of the eldest brother went to be with his brothers in the sky. Each night the Seven Star Brothers, together again, dance high above the council house of the Seneca People, and this story is told.

How the Animals
Came to Be of Many Colors

*A story of the Kathlamet People of the Pacific
Northwest*

When the world first began, all the animals were
the same color as the earth, all shades of brown.
But when they looked at the reflection of the sun in
water, they saw all the colors of the Sky Man's Bow
that shows when it has rained. They wished they could
have clothes of all those pretty colors. They wanted to
shoot the sun with an arrow, to bring it down to earth.

They wanted to kill the sun and take its clothes of
many colors. Some animals got in a canoe and paddled
out to sea to try to get closer to the sun, but they came
back disappointed. Others climbed high mountains to
try to get a good shot at it, but their arrows always fell
back to earth without reaching the sun. Still others hid
under the bushes or in the ground, afraid of what might
happen if the sun was shot and fell to earth. The last
animals flew high up into the air to try to shoot the

sun, but their arrows always missed.

Blue Jay was the thinker among the animals that flew, the birds, and he told all the animals, "We must shoot the sun so that we may have its clothes of many colors. We will shoot again tomorrow."

The next day, Blue Jay went out with the other animals to shoot at the sun, but he sent his two daughters to look in the woods for the roots of the potentilla plant, used as a medicine and in ceremonies.

The girls could hear the animals far away on the shore, talking and shooting at the sun above the water. The younger sister said, "I wish we could have a chance at shooting the sun." The older sister dug and said nothing.

A little later, the younger sister said again, "I wish we could have a chance at shooting the sun." Again the sister dug and did not reply. The younger sister spoke a third and a fourth time, and the older sister did not answer. The fifth time the younger spoke, the older answered, "Father has many arrows."

The girls dug on in silence.

The next morning they awoke early and took their baskets to gather potentilla root, but into the baskets they slipped some of father Blue Jay's arrows, and they took two of his older bows that he never used anymore. They went into the woods and made clothing of leaves to wear over their bird clothing. They tied their hair up the way young men wear it.

They went down to the shore at midday and joined the others shooting at the sun. Everyone wondered who they were. The older sister shot so well she almost hit the sun, and the younger sister came even closer.

But no one hit the sun, and they all went home. The sisters went into the woods, took off their coats, and dug roots to take home.

The next day, the strange young men were back at the shore, and they came closer to shooting the sun than anyone else. When the sisters got back to their lodge, they heard all the animals talking about who the strange youths in leaf coats were. Blue Jay looked hard at his daughters, but he said nothing.

On the third day, the strange youths were again on the shore, and all the animals tried to shoot the sun. The older youth in strange clothing almost hit the sun. But the last arrow shot by the younger of the strange youths hit the sun, and a great piece of it fell to the sea.

The two strange youths jumped in a canoe and paddled out and picked up the shiny piece of the sun. It shone in all the colors that reflect off the water. They came ashore and ran into the woods carrying the piece of rainbow-colored sun. It was rightfully theirs, but all the animals had hoped that they would share.

On the fourth day, when the sisters went out very early to bathe, Blue Jay searched the lodge and found his old bows and some of his arrows missing. When his daughters came back, he faced them.

"Where are my old bows, and why are so many arrows gone? Where is the piece of the sun?"

"Take your bath, and then we will tell you," said the older sister.

After Blue Jay took his bath, they told him everything. They went into the woods and brought out the piece of the sun, which they had hidden in a basket. Blue Jay gathered all the animals on the shore, and there he cut the piece of the sun into many smaller pieces so that each animal could have a bite to eat. Each animal became the color or colors of the little piece they ate. Some animals became one solid color, and others had stripes of color, and some even had more than one color. Blue Jay greedily saved the biggest piece for himself. He took one bite and became bright blue. He was about to take another bite, and become all the colors of the rainbow, when Clam jumped up off the sand and grabbed the piece and ate it down.

Clam may be the slowest of the animals of the water, but on his shell he carries all the colors of the rainbow. All the other animals wear their own new colors to this day. And Blue Jay and all his family are blue, blue and blue, for that was the only bite he took of the rainbow piece of the sun.

Trickster Stories

The tricksters in Native American stories are child-like in their innocence and playfulness, in their curiosity and their way of getting into trouble. But they are very adult-like in the way they face the problems and monsters of life, and their tricks are often played for a good reason. We admire their wit and wisdom, their clever ideas, and the way they survive any test of survival. But we don't admire everything they do, because they often show us through their antics the kind of behavior we should be smart enough to avoid.

Here are stories about the tricksters.

Kulóskap and
the Three Wishes

*A story of the Micmac and Passamaquoddy People of
New England*

Kulóskap the trickster gave the People many gifts
in the ancient times, from the use of fire to ways
of making pottery and baskets. When the People were
gathered into a proper village and daily life in the
village was underway, Kulóskap went away from the
People. But he did not yet leave the earth; instead he
wandered around the world of the People. The People
missed Kulóskap, and he sent his servants the loons to
fly everywhere the People were, and sing to them that
Kulóskap was still on the earth, and whosoever would
search for him could find him, and he would give that
person one wish.

Three young men decided to go and seek
Kulóskap. They wandered the forest together for
seven years, looking for the trickster who granted
wishes. They heard his hunting dogs baying one night,

and went toward the sound. The three followed the distant baying by night for three months before they came to Kulóskap's lodge.

Kulóskap welcomed the men warmly, and they had a great feast. Later that night, Kulóskap asked each of the men what they wished for.

The first said, "I wish to become a great hunter, and a master at catching game. In this way, I will feed my family and my village."

Kulóskap gave this man a flute that played a song so beautiful that all the animals of the forest would come to its song. The young hunter took the flute and thanked Kulóskap. He left and started on the long path to his village.

The second said, "I wish to become a great ladies' man, and a master at winning the hearts of young maidens. In this way I will have many companions and many wives to make me happy."

Kulóskap smiled and asked, "How many wives do you wish for?"

The young man thought and answered, "enough, and more than enough." Kulóskap gave him a bark bundle tied tightly with deer sinew.

"Do not open this bundle until you reach your lodge," said Kulóskap, smiling again. The young lover took the bundle, thanked the trickster, and left on the long path to his village.

The third young man said, "I love a good joke. All my friends laugh at the funny things I say. I wish to know the magic sound that will make everyone laugh as they have never laughed before."

Kulóskap laughed and gave the young joker a root

which, when eaten, gave the eater the power to make a magic sound that made everyone laugh. "Do not eat this root until you reach your village," warned Kulóskap. The young man thanked the trickster and left on the long path to his village.

The young hunter, when he was almost home, played on his flute and all the animals of the forest came to the song. The hunter took what he needed to feed his family, thanked the animals, and went to his lodge. He never went without venison to eat or a bear rug to sleep under, and with his flute the village was warm and well-fed for many winters to come.

The young lover, when he was almost home, gave in to curiosity. He sat down and opened the bark bundle. Out came a beautiful woman who kissed him. As she hugged him tight, another came out of the bundle, then another. Soon so many were kissing and hugging him that he could not breath. Wandering hunters found his corpse, but the women from the bundle were never seen again.

The young joker, when he was almost home, gave in to curiosity. He took the root, ate it, and gave a loud burp. The owls in the tree laughed and laughed at the sound. When the young joker arrived home, he burped so loudly the entire village came running and laughing. The young joker couldn't hunt—his burps scared the animals away. He could not sing at the campfire—his burps interrupted the singing. No one could sleep in his lodge—his burps kept everyone awake and laughing.

Finally, the joker went away and became the bullfrog Aklibimo, burping happily all night long.

Raccoon and the Crabs

*A story of the Algonquian and Iroquoian People of
New England and the Atlantic Seaboard*

Raccoon the Trickster was walking along in the forest, and he was getting very hungry. Every time he tried to catch some freshwater crabs, the little crabs got away from him, so he hadn't even tried this day. The path through the forest led alongside the stream, and Raccoon saw the little crabs looking at him with their funny eyes. The crabs' eyes stuck above the water like frogs' eyes, and they could see Raccoon coming. As Raccoon got closer to the stream bank, the crabs dropped below the surface of the water.

Raccoon decided to play a trick on the crabs.

"I am a dead man," groaned Raccoon. "I have had nothing to eat for days and days. I'm so weak I can't even catch any little crabs!" Raccoon began to sway from side to side as if he were weak with hunger. One or two pairs of crab eyes came back up to look when Raccoon began to stagger.

"I am a dead man," said Raccoon, and he fell face

first into the mud of the stream bank. He lay there without moving for a long time.

Two by two the crabs' eyes popped up to the surface of the stream and stared at Raccoon. Two crabs went down to the crabs' lodge and got the sachem, the head man of the crab village. The sachem, whose name was Hasanowane, came to the surface and looked.

The crabs looked at Raccoon for a long time. Raccoon never moved. At last Hasanowane sent two crab warriors to see if Raccoon was really dead. The crabs sidled up to Raccoon and poked him with their tiny claws. Raccoon did not move.

At last the crab sachem came out of the water and all the little Crab People followed him. They began to dance around Raccoon in a circle, and sang a victory song.

Many of the crab warriors climbed up on Raccoon's back and danced. Their little feet tickled him, but Raccoon didn't move. Finally the sachem of the crabs stood up high on his little legs and made a speech.

"Let us now eat Raccoon, who has eaten so many of us in years past," said Hasanowane.

All the little crabs gathered around Raccoon and got ready to take a bite.

Just then Raccoon jumped up, muddy but alive, and began to grab up the crabs. He was so hungry and in such a hurry that he didn't even bother to wash his food as he usually does. He ate and ate and ate. He had a great feast of crabs that day.

But he never got all the mud off his face, and his eyes have dark circles around them still today!

Coyote and the Rock

A story of many Southwestern and Western tribes

One fine day Coyote was out for a walk. It had been cold that morning, and Coyote was wearing his favorite blanket to keep him warm. As the sun walked high into the sky, on his daily journey, Coyote began to get too warm. Finally, Coyote began to sweat.

"This blanket is too warm to wear," said Coyote, who often talked to himself. "I don't want to carry it around with me all day! I think I'll give it away."

Walking along the trail, Coyote passed a huge rock that stood at the edge of a steep downhill slope. He took off his blanket.

"Grandfather Rock," said Coyote, "I wish to make you a gift." Coyote took off his blanket and, with a fancy flip of the ends, he laid it ceremoniously on the huge rock. "I am glad to make this give away, for this blanket will keep you warm for many winters to come. I hope you like it!" The rock said ... nothing.

"Don't bother to thank me," said Coyote as he climbed up the trail. The rock said ... nothing. Coyote stretched his long, long legs and climbed higher, for in those days Coyote's legs were as long and graceful as Antelope's. "Goodbye, Grandfather!" called Coyote. The rock said ... nothing.

Coyote went along the mesa rim all day, getting into trouble, and putting his nose in other animals' business. By sundown, it was getting cold, and Coyote started to shiver.

"Brrrr," said Coyote out loud. "Where's that blanket of mine?" Just about then Coyote came down the trail to the huge rock and saw his blanket. "There it is!" he yelped, and ran to it.

Coyote took hold of one end of the blanket and pulled. The other end was hung up on a sharp outcropping. Coyote pulled and pulled, but his blanket wouldn't come loose.

"Give me back my blanket, you stupid old rock!" yelped Coyote, completely forgetting that he had given it away in the heat of the day. "Are you going to give me that blanket?" asked Coyote angrily. The rock said ... nothing.

Coyote in haste and anger, came around to the downhill side of the rock, and jumped up, grabbing the other end of the blanket. Now the uphill end was caught on the rock. Coyote gave a good yank, and the blanket came free.

"That's more like it," snarled Coyote, wrapping the blanket around him, and starting down the mesa slope. Then the rock spoke.

"Groan," said the rock.

Coyote's yellow eyes got wide.

"Groan," said the rock.

Coyote turned back to look at the rock.

"Groan," said the rock, leaning downhill towards Coyote.

"Yipe," said Coyote meekly.

"Groan," said the rock, and it began to roll toward Coyote. Coyote ran as fast as he could, his blanket flying out behind him. The rock rolled down the mesa slope, end-over-end, singing its own deadly song.

The rock slowly gained on Coyote; even Coyote's long, graceful legs couldn't get him away fast enough. One end of the rock caught the blanket and Coyote flipped over.

"Crunch" said the rock—or was it Coyote?—as the rock rolled over poor Coyote, squashing him flat as frybread.

The rock rolled on, taking the blanket with it.

Coyote lay there moaning long after the echoes of the rock had ended. The valley was silent. The moon came up, and Coyote sang a sad, sad song to it.

Slowly Coyote lifted himself up on his now very short, bent, and scrunched-up legs. His tongue hung out as he trotted somewhat sideways—as coyotes have trotted ever since—down to the rock in the valley floor. The rock lay on its side in the moonlight. It was sleeping on the blanket. Only the very corners of the blanket showed out from under the rock.

Coyote stood there for a long time looking at his blanket.

"I never liked that blanket anyway," snorted Coyote, and he loped off along the valley floor under the full moon.

Possum's Beautiful Tail

A story of the Cherokee People of Oklahoma, North Carolina, and Georgia

In the old days, Possum had the most beautiful tail of all the animals. It was covered with long, silky hair, and Possum liked nothing better than to wave it around when the Animal People met together in council. He would hold up his tail and show it to the Animal People.

"You see my tail?" he would say. "Is it not the most beautiful tail you have ever seen? Surely it is finer than any other animals'."

He was so proud of his tail that the other animals became tired of hearing him brag about it. Finally, Rabbit decided to do something about it. Rabbit was the messenger of the animals, and he is the one who always told them when there was going to be a council meeting. He went to Possum's house.

"My friend," Rabbit said, "there is going to be a great meeting. Our chief, Bear, wants you to sit next to him in council. He wants you to be the first one to speak, because you have such a beautiful tail."

Possum was flattered. "It is true," he said, "one who has such a beautiful tail as I should be the first to speak in council." He held up his tail, combing it with his long fingers. "Is not my tail the most wonderful thing you have ever seen?"

Rabbit looked close at Possums' tail. "My friend," Rabbit said, "it looks to me as though your tail is just a *little* dirty. I think it would look even better if you would allow me to clean it. I have some special medicine that would make your tail look just the way it should look."

Possum looked closely at his tail. It did seem as if it was a little bit dirty. "Yes," said Possum, "that is a good idea. I want all the animals to admire my tail when I speak in council."

Then Rabbit mixed up his medicine. It was *very* strong. So strong that it loosened all the hair on Possum's tail. But as he put the medicine on Possum's tail, he wrapped the tail in skin that had been shed by a snake.

"This snakeskin will make sure the medicine works well," Rabbit said. "Do not take it off until you speak in council tomorrow. Then the People will all see your tail just as it should be seen."

Possum did as Rabbit said. He kept the snakeskin wrapped tightly around his tail all through the night. The next day, when the animals met for council, Possum sat next to Chief Bear. As soon as the meeting began, he stood up to speak.

As he spoke he walked back and forth beside the council fire, swinging his tail that was wrapped in snakeskin. Everyone was looking at Possum's tail. Possum grinned with pride. The time was right. He began to unwrap his tail and bragged that he had been chosen to speak first at council because of his beautiful tail.

"I am proud," he said, "to speak first and show off my beautiful tail." With that he let the snakeskin unravel and fall to the ground. Along with the snakeskin, all the hair on his tail also fell off. Rabbit had tricked him. His tail was ugly and hairless, and everyone was looking right at him.

The grin froze on his face. He was so embarrassed!

Possum fell down on the ground and pretended to be dead. He did not move again until everyone had finished speaking at council and had left, laughing.

To this day, Possum still has that silly grin frozen on his face. And if he feels threatened or embarrassed, he falls down and plays dead.

Raven and Octopus Woman

A story of the Skagit, Nootka, and other Pacific Northwest tribes

Raven was such a pest! He was always getting into other people's business, always asking silly questions, and he always thought he knew everything. One day he was flying along over the bay, and he saw that the tide was out. He thought he might go down to the beach at low tide and see what he could see.

Octopus Woman was moving down the beach, with a basket on her back, and a yew-wood digging stick in one of her hands. She was going to dig for clams. She put the clams in her basket. Raven came down and began to walk around and ask silly questions.

"Octopus Woman, what are you doing? Are you digging for clams? Huh?" said Raven, "Huh?" Octopus Woman ignored Raven and continued to dig.

Raven came closer and tilted his head from side to side. "Are you digging for clams, Octopus Woman? Is that what you are doing? Huh?" Octopus woman did not look up. She kept digging and the tide began to slowly come in.

"Are you digging for clams, Octopus Woman?" cawed Raven, looking in her basket. "Looks like clams, huh?" Octopus woman stopped digging for just a moment, then went back to work, ignoring Raven.

Raven poked his beak right down into Octopus Woman's basket and said rather rudely, "Looks like clams. Are you digging for clams? Huh?"

Suddenly Octopus woman turned and looked right into Raven's face. Raven leaned back, startled. She dropped her digging stick and wrapped one of her arms around Raven's neck. "Raven, I'm so glad to see you." She wrapped another arm around his neck, and said, "And I'm so glad that you are interested in what I am doing."

The tide was rising higher as Octopus Woman wrapped another arm around Raven's waist. And to answer your question, yes! I am digging clams." The tide came in up around Raven's ankles.

"I see," said Raven, rather meekly.

"Yes, it is clams that I am digging, and I am digging these clams for supper." Another arm went around Raven's waist as the sea water rose around his knees.

"I see, I see," said Raven. "Well, goodbye now." He tried to move, but he was held fast by Octopus Woman's arms. Another arm went around one of Raven's wings. The water was coming up to Raven's waist.

"Yours was a very good question, Raven," said Octopus Woman, wrapping another arm around Raven's other wing. "And it deserves a good answer. I was digging clams when you came along."

"Well, thank you for answering me, Octopus Woman," said Raven, "And now I must go." The tide was up to his chest. Under the water, Octopus Woman wrapped another arm around Raven's leg.

"No, no, Raven," said Octopus Woman, wrapping her last arm around Raven's other leg. "Why don't you stay for supper?" The water came up around Raven's neck.

"What's for supper?" asked Raven weakly.

"You are," said Octopus Woman.

"I see," said Raven, and they disappeared below the waves.

Luckily for Raven, he has many lives and always seems to come back.

The Spirit World

For Native American People, the spirit world is very close to our world, and many of their stories reflect that closeness. In stories about ancient times, People and animals could pass back and forth between the spirit world and our world. Even today, some tribes say, People in our world can speak with and learn from the spirits of People and animals in the spirit world.

Ghost of the White Deer

A story of the Chickasaw People of Oklahoma

A brave, young warrior of the Chickasaw Nation fell in love with the daughter of a chief. The chief did not like the young man, who was called Blue Jay. So the chief invented a price for the bride that he was sure that Blue Jay could not pay.

"Bring me the hide of the white deer," said the chief. The Chickasaws believed that animals that were all-white were magical. "The price for my daughter is one white deer." Then the chief laughed. The chief knew that an all-white deer, an albino, was very rare and would be very hard to find. White deerskin was the best material to use in a wedding dress, and the best white deer skin came from the albino deer.

Blue Jay went to his beloved, whose name was Bright Moon. "I will return with your bride price in one moon, and we will be married. This I promise you." Taking his best bow and his sharpest arrows, Blue Jay began to hunt.

Three weeks went by, and Blue Jay was often

hungry, lonely, and scratched by briars. Then, one night during a full moon, Blue Jay saw a white deer that seemed to drift through the moonlight. When the deer was very close to where Blue Jay hid, he shot his sharpest arrow. The arrow sank deep into the deer's heart. But instead of sinking to his knees to die, the deer began to run. And instead of running away, the deer began to run toward Blue Jay, his red eyes glowing, his horns sharp and menacing.

A month passed and Blue Jay did not return as he had promised Bright Moon. As the months dragged by, the tribe decided that he would never return.

But Bright Moon never took any other young man as a husband, for she had a secret. When the moon was shining as brightly as her name, Bright Moon would often see the white deer in the smoke of the campfire, running, with an arrow in his heart. She lived hoping the deer would finally fall, and Blue Jay would return.

To this day the white deer is sacred to the Chickasaw People, and the white deerskin is still the favorite material for the wedding dress.

Dance of the Dead

A story of the Luiseño People of southern California

Once a year the People of Kamak left their village and went up Palomar Mountain to gather acorns. Everyone went, young and old, and even the ill were carried along on litters so that the village could stay together at this important time. The houses were left empty; no one was afraid of thieves in those days.

While the village was deserted, a man from another nearby village called Ahoya came to Kamak. He found everyone gone. He knew where they had gone, and why, so he knew he could not see his friends on this trip. He decided to spend the night and go on his way the next morning. He did not go into anyone's house, but rather he took a large basket normally used to store grain and turned it over. He crawled under the basket, where the wind could not bother him. He fell asleep.

In the early evening, but long after dark, he was awakened by someone calling People out to dance. At first he thought the People of Kamak had come back from acorn-gathering. Then, being an old man, he began to recognize the voices of People he had known many years ago, but who were now long dead. He began to realize that the voices were spirits of the Dead! While the People of Kamak were away, the Dead had returned to dance.

The old man lay quietly under the basket, listening to the voices of all the People, all the way back to the ancient days. He heard the Woman-who-was-turned-into-rock as she sang. He heard the Man-who-scooped-rock-with-his-hand as he sang. All the People of the ancient days were here in the village again.

The old man could not stand to wait any longer. After he had listened for hours, he wanted to look at the People he had known as a young man and the faces of the People he had only heard about in the old stories. He threw the basket off and looked where the Dead had been dancing.

There was only a flock of birds, and they flew away, startled by the basket overturning. The turtle-shell rattle the Dead had played all night as they danced lay on the ground. It was now just a piece of soaproot.

The old man was not allowed to see the Dance of the Dead.

The Girl Who Married a Ghost

A story of the Chinook and Klickitat People of the Pacific Northwest

In a village of log lodges alongside the Great Water lived Lone Feather, the chief and the son of a chief. Lone Feather loved a girl named Robin. The day Robin had been born, a robin sang outside her father's lodge, and she was given that name. Lone Feather was named when, on the day of his birth, he pulled a single feather from the headdress of his father, the old chief.

Lone Feather and Robin planned to marry in the springtime, when the snows in the Cascade Mountains melted. But in the last cold days of winter, Lone Feather took sick and died of a fever. His spirit left his body and walked down the trail of the spirits to the Land of the Dead. Robin and all the village wept and grieved at the loss of the young chief.

The villagers took Lone Feather's body by canoe to the Island of the Dead, and placed it on a burial platform. Then they left quickly before the sun went down. No one dared to stay on the Island of the Dead after sundown, for fear they might lose their way and become one of the Dead.

In the springtime, Robin had a dream. She dreamed that the spirit of Lone Feather spoke to her. His spirit told her that he had not found peace in the Land of the Dead because he missed her so much. When the sun rose, Robin told her father of her dream. At first he refused to listen to her, but at last he gave in and agreed to her plan.

When the sun was high, Robin and her father paddled their canoe up the Great River to the most distant and most ancient island of burial. No one went to this island at all anymore. It had become the most secret and most sacred place of the Dead.

A low fog hung over the island, and Robin's father became afraid. They brought the canoe up on the gravel shore of the island, and they embraced and said good-bye. Robin's father paddled away alone and only looked back once as the fog closed in on the island and the sun set. Robin made her way inland on the island, picking her way through deep ferns and vines among the trees.

As it grew darker and darker, she could hear drums playing in the distance. She began to hear People singing. At last she came to the Village of the Dead. The People seemed very happy, singing and dancing in a circle around a warm fire. When she entered the clearing, they came to greet her. At first they were very friendly to her, but then they began to see that she was still alive. They began to step back and shy away from her.

"No one who is alive is allowed to come to the

Land of the Dead," said a wise old woman. "You must return to your own People."

Just then Lone Feather came into the clearing and saw Robin. They ran into each other's arms and were happy to be together again. Lone Feather looked more healthy and handsome than he had the last days of his life among the living.

All of the Dead liked and respected Lone Feather, and they agreed to allow Robin to live among them. They sang and danced all night long. Just before the sun came up, they all went to their lodges and laid down on their sleeping mats. Robin and Lone Feather went to his house. The robins were singing as they went to sleep.

Robin was not used to sleeping when the sun was high, and she awoke at about the high point of the sun in the sky. She turned and looked at her handsome husband. In the bright light of day, the sleeping mat was rotten and crumbling. The lodge was falling into ruin. The handsome young chief was a skeleton. Robin jumped up and ran outside. All around the decaying village were skeletons, lying where one of the Dead had stood or sat or lain when the sun caught them.

The houses of the Dead were rotting logs. The canoes of the Dead were dried and torn and full of holes. The salmon she had seen them catch the night before were nothing but dead leaves that had floated on the waters of the Great River. Robin sat alone all day, very much afraid.

As the sun set, she saw the skeletons become whole People again. They sat up and talked, they stood up and sang. Someone began to build a fire. Men went out in the canoes, which looked new and well-made in the firelight. They brought in nets of fresh salmon and cooked them over the fire. Lone Feather came looking for Robin, and they were happy again.

Robin slept all day long after that and was only awake when the Dead were awake, in darkness. Months later, Lone Feather and Robin had a son. They were all very happy, but Robin wished she could visit her father and mother in the Land of the Living. She wanted them to see their new grandson.

All of the Dead warned Robin not to go back to the Living.

"If you do go back," said the wise old woman, whose name was Owl Woman, "you must not allow anyone to look upon the child for ten days."

Another said, "If you go back to the Land of the Living, they may not let you return here."

Still another one said, "If you go back to the Land of the Living, they may think you are an evil ghost. They may not welcome you back. They may not even let you back into the village."

In spite of the good advice from her friends among the Dead, Robin went back to her own village. She wrapped her son in a blanket and waited for sunrise. When the Dead were all skeletons, she took the best of the canoes, patched its holes herself, and paddled back to her home. At her village, the People did not trust her. They thought she was an evil ghost. No one ever came back from the Dead. What business did *she* have coming back?

Robin's father and mother were glad to see her. She hid in their house so the other People would not be angered by the sight of her. Robin's mother wanted badly to see her grandson, but Robin told her what Owl Woman had said: no one of the Living must look on the child for ten days.

One bright day, while Robin was asleep, her mother opened the blanket up to look at the baby. The baby was just a skeleton. The woman screamed and dropped the tiny bones. Day and night, the bones were just bones; the baby was never to be seen by his grandmother.

Sadly, Robin gathered the tiny bones and wrapped them in the blanket. She hugged her father and mother goodbye forever and paddled back up the Great River to the Island of the Dead. The sun went down, and the canoe came aground near the Village of the Dead. Inside his blanket, the baby cried.

Robin, Lone Feather, and their son were happy together. The Dead met in tribal council and declared that no one may ever again pass back and forth between the Land of the Living and the Land of the Dead.

Acknowledgments

The editors of this collection are indebted to Teresa Pijoan of Algodones, New Mexico, and to all the other storytellers listed in the individual story notes. We offer them all our sincere thanks.

We are also indebted to the late Claude Medford, Choctaw basket maker; Anna Mitchell, Cherokee potter; Woodrow Hainey, Seminole storyteller and flute maker; Bobby Lankford, Mescalero Apache drummaker; Pam Davis, Nez Percé beadworker; Lee Price Yee, Cherokee artisan; Michael Blue Hawk Adams and Belinda Morningstar Adams, living history re-enactors; Joe and Patty Mooney, Cherokee crafts-persons; and Jim Fire Eagle, elder and shaman in the Uto-Aztecan tribe of Kansas, and his wife Marion Snowflower. Each of these Native American guided us in our search for stories.

While many of the stories that we tell personally are from our own tribal heritages (see the preface), we also tell stories from other tribes with the consent of the tellers who provided a variant of the story to us. We have heard many stories from professional and traditional storytellers, but we have included in this collection only stories that are non-sacred, and that we have heard aloud two or more times, often from members of different tribes. The tribal origins of the stories, given at the beginning of each story, are approximate because stories are often told by more than one tribe and many intertribal variants exist.

All of the stories in this collection are retold; storytellers dealing with non-sacred stories tend to retell events of the narrative in their own words and at their own level of grammaticality, sometimes altering details in order to fit the audience or circumstances.

A few of these stories are "ours," that is, we learned them in childhood from family, and some came from informal story swaps at Silver Dollar City, Missouri; for these stories, exact source notes are unavailable. For most of the stories, however, we provide oral and written sources in the following notes.

Notes

The narratives in this anthology were heard, learned, or collected between 1952 and 1993. As more tribal councils have moved to restrict the use and telling of the stories of their particular tribe or band, we have researched each story from written sources that were collected, sometimes more than a century ago, with the approval of previous tribal councils. Since 1981 we have spent hundreds of hours in the libraries of Memphis State University, Arkansas Tech University and in the Mullins Library of the University of Arkansas at Fayetteville corroborating the stories we have heard with recorded variants. We have done this research in order to confirm the origin of the stories, to fill in lacunae (missing elements from incomplete oral renditions), verify details that vary from variant to variant, and confirm that the story is in the public domain and is not the intrinsic property of a specific teller.

The collection and preservation of Native American oral narratives by non-Indians began before the United States was founded as a nation (a development which the Iroquois chieftains recommended because they were tired of negotiating separate treaties with separate British colonies). Such organizations as the Carnegie Institute and the Field Museum sponsored story research in the 1800s. But the finest collection work was done by the Bureau of American Ethnology of the Smithsonian Institution which, between the years 1887 and 1971, published forty-eight *Annual Reports* (which will be abbreviated as *BAEAR*) and two hundred *Bulletins* (*BAEB*). We have cited these publications by abbreviation and volume number.

1. **The Twin Brothers** we first heard at the Native American Gathering at Lake Ouachita State Park, Hot Springs, Arkansas, on June 15, 1989. A Caddo named Wing told this story to George A. Dorsey, who published it in his *Traditions of the Caddo* (Washington: Carnegie Institution, 1905) p. 31.

2. **Grandmother Spider Steals the Fire** was told to us at Chuckalissa Mounds, Memphis, Tennessee, on August 2, 1988 by Kenneth Willis, a Mississippi Choctaw craftsman, and Grady John, a Mississippi Choctaw storyteller and potter. The similar Cherokee version is found in Mooney's *Myths of the Cherokee*, *BAEAR* 19:2.

3. **Old Man at the Beginning** we first heard at a story swap in Tulsa, Oklahoma, November 9, 1991, told by a young Crow Indian whose name we did not learn. For details, we sought out "The Origin Myth" in S.C. Simms' *Traditions of the Crow*, Field Columbian Museum Anthropological Series, pub. 85, vol. 2, no. 6 (Chicago: Field Columbian Museum, 1903) p. 281.

4. **Race with Buffalo** was first told to us by Teresa Pijoan, December 31, 1988, at Placitas, New Mexico, in our annual New Year's Eve story swap around the *horno* fireplace. New Year's Eve is a crack in time, and a good hour for storytelling and lighting the *luminaria*. After hearing the story again in Tulsa in 1991, we sought out "The Race" in George Bird Grinnell's *By Cheyenne Campfires* (New Haven: Yale University Press, 1926) p. 252. In Grinnell's translation, the buffalo runner is Slim-Walking-Woman.

5. **Blue Corn Maiden and the Coming of Winter** was first heard by Richard from a curio shop owner in Albuquerque, New Mexico, during the summer of 1967. We found the Acoma variant in summary in Hamilton A. Tyler's *Pueblo Gods and Myths* (Norman: University of Oklahoma Press, 1964) pp. 166-8. The Eight Northern Pueblos version heard in 1967 was also published in *New Mexico* magazine in the early 1960s.

6. **Bears' Lodge** is the best-known Indian story in Wyoming and Montana, told by the Cheyenne, the Lakota (Sioux), and the Kiowa. Our variant most closely resembles the Kiowa story, in which *Tso' Ai'* ("Bears' Lodge") is Devil's Tower, America's first national monument, and the Seven Sisters become the constellation we call the Pleiades. This story was first told to Judy in a story swap at Silver Dollar City in the summer of 1990. Our current variant was first provided by Ken Teutsch of Casper, Wyoming on November 23, 1990, with other details added by a member of the Kiowa Tribe after hearing us tell the story at the McHaffie Homestead in 1992. The Lakota (Sioux) version of the story can be found in Ella E. Clark's *Indian Legends from the Northern Rockies* (Norman: University of Oklahoma Press, 1966) p. 305.

7. **The Evening Star** was first told to us by park rangers who had heard it at the previous day's storytelling at the Native American Gathering at Lake Ouachita State Park, Hot Springs, Arkansas, June 16, 1990. We also found the version told by an unidentified informant to George A. Dorsey and published in his *Traditions of the Caddo* (Washington: Carnegie Institution, 1905) p. 26.

8. **The Flying Head** was first told to us by Teresa Pijoan, December 31, 1987, at the first *horno* storytelling session held by our families. Other versions appear in the *BAEAR* 2, Vol. 2, p. 59, and in *Legends of the Iroquois told by "The Cornplanter"* compiled by W. W. Canfield and published in 1902. Although "The Cornplanter," known as Gar-yan-wah-ga in the Seneca language, generally hated European-Americans for the treachery of the wars of the late 1700s, he did have a few "white" friends whom he trusted, and with whom he shared his stories. "The Cornplanter" (1732?-1836) told of a Flying Head with black wings and small, sharp claws. The young woman in the New England version of the story was roasting acorns on the hearth and tricked the Head into eating red-hot coals. As the story moved across the continent with the Seneca People, the acorns became bread, more closely matching Southwestern traditions.

9. **Skunnee Wundee and the Stone Giant** is a variant of the stories found in *Seneca Myths and Folktales* collected by A.C. Parker (Buffalo: Buffalo Historical Society, 1923) story #53, p. 334. Stories about Skunnee Wundee and another character named Hoot-Owl were favorites of Richard's, told to him in the early 1950s by his father, Dr. Morgan M. Young, an educator and storyteller. Skunnee Wundee, which is spelled six different ways depending on

how the Seneca word is transliterated into English letters, means "Cross-the-Creek" or "Beyond-the-Rapids."

10. **The Turkey Girl** we first heard at a story swap at Oliver LaFarge Library in Santa Fé, New Mexico, in December, 1987. Other versions appear in *Tewa Tales* by Elsie C. Parson in *Memoirs of the American Folk-lore Society*, Vol. XIX (New York: A.F.S., 1926), story #36, p. 118, and in *Memoirs of the American Anthropological Association* (Washington: A.A.A.., 1935) #43 in "The Pueblo of Santo Domingo, New Mexico" by Leslie A. White, pp. 191-4.

11. **Long Hair and Flint Bird** we learned from Wolf Robe Hunt, then of Catoosa, Oklahoma, formerly of the Ácoma Pueblo, son of Chief Day Break. The Young family first met the Hunt family in 1952, in New Mexico, but the story was learned in 1981. The story is a superior variant of "Kasewat Rescues His Wife From Flint Bird" in Leslie A. White's "The Ácoma Indians," *BAEAR* 47, p. 172.

12. **The Bloodsucker** was first told to us by Teresa Pijoan on December 31, 1988, in Placitas, New Mexico, at our annual storytelling.

13. **Bear's Race With Turtle** we first heard, to the best of our memory, at a powwow in Tulsa, Oklahoma in the 1970s. Many versions exist, such as the one in *BAEAR* 32, p. 229.

14. **Cricket and Cougar** we first heard at a story swap at the McHaffie Homestead at Silver Dollar City in July of 1992. Following a lead, we found Katherine Chandler's *In the Reign of Coyote* (Boston: Ginn and Company, 1905) with this story on p. 34.

15. **The Two Sisters' Husband** we first heard at a story swap at Cahokia Mounds in Collinsville, Illinois, on September 20, 1987. George A. Dorsey's *Traditions of the Caddo* (Washington: Carnegie Institution, 1905) includes a version told by Wing, an Oklahoma Caddo on p. 67. The Seneca variant "Owl and the Two Sisters" is found in *BAEAR* 32, p. 150.

16. **The Ball Game Between the Animals and the Birds** we first heard at Cahokia Mounds in Collinsville, Illinois on September 25, 1988. However, this version was provided to us by Alonzo Great Thunderbird Combs, a Cherokee artisan of Malvern, Arkansas. The story can be found in *BAEAR* 19: 1, p. 286.

17. **Where the Dog Ran Across the Sky** we first heard in Cherokee, North Carolina, in July of 1982. This version was

provided by Great Thunderbird Combs (see no. 16) in the winter of 1991.

18. **How Bear Lost His Tail** Richard first heard in childhood from his father (see no. 9) and also appears in *BAEAR* 2: 2, p. 77, and in M.C. Judd's *Wigwam Stories* (Boston: Ginn and Company, 1912) p. 112.

19. **Coyote's Sad Song to the Moon** Richard first heard from a curio shop owner in Albuquerque, New Mexico, in the summer of 1967. We found the Zuñi version in Hamilton A. Tyler's *Pueblo Animals and Myths* (Norman: University of Oklahoma Press, 1975) p. 165. The Eight Northern Pueblos version was also published in *New Mexico* magazine in the early 1960s.

20. **Kanati the Hunter and the Cave of Animals** we first heard in Cherokee, North Carolina, in July, 1982. This version was provided by Great Thunderbird Combs (see no. 16) in the winter of 1991.

21. **How Buzzard Got His Clothing** we first heard at a powwow-style story swap on the grounds of Silver Dollar City at the Indian encampment of the Olde Country Folk Festival in May of 1984. The story is also found in *Legends of the Iroquois told by "The Cornplanter"* (see no. 8). In the Cornplanter's version, the birds tease Buzzard afterwards, and he points out that he had his choice of all the clothing in the world and chose what he wears today.

22. **The Seven Star Brothers** we first heard at a story swap in Oklahoma City, January 26, 1991. Variants are found in the *BAEAR* 2:2, p. 62, and in A. C. Parker's *Seneca Myths and Folktales* (Buffalo: Buffalo Historical Society, 1923) story #5, p. 83.

23. **How the Animals Came to be of Many Colors** we first heard in Jonesborough, Tennessee, in October of 1983, swapping stories in front of the Taylor House. We heard it again in July of 1992 at the McHaffie Homestead. The story is also found in Franz Boas' *Kathlamet Texts*, *BAEB* 26, p. 39.

24. **Kulóscap and the Three Wishes** is retold from *Kulóscap the Master* translated by C. G. Leland and J. D. Prince (New York: Funk and Wagnalls, 1902) p. 64. We have heard many stories of Kulóscap, Glooskap or Glooskabi, as he is known to different tribes, many of which have overlapping narratives. This story was first given to us in fragmentary form in 1987, and is largely the result of reconstruction and research.

25. **Raccoon and the Crabs** Richard first heard in childhood, though he later doubted his memory after hearing different variants involving crawfish, and the African-American "Br'er Rabbit Fools the Frogs." The crab variant, however, is found in A. C. Parker's *Seneca Myths and Folktales* (Buffalo: Buffalo Historical Society, 1923) story # 46, p. 319, and the crawfish variant is found in *BAEAR* 32, p. 229.

26. **Coyote and the Rock** was first told to us by a teenage Dogrib Apache woman named Jane during a story swap at Cahokia Mounds, Collinsville, Illinois, on September 20, 1987. Other variants are found as "Rolling Rock" from the Montana Flathead tribe, collected by Louisa McDermott and published in the *Journal of American Folk-lore*, 1901, p. 245, and as "The Offended Rolling Stone" from the Pawnee in Stith Thompson's *Tales of North American Indians* (Bloomington: Indiana University Press, [1929] 1966) p. 64.

27. **Possum's Beautiful Tail** is a story we have heard so many times we are unable to remember where we first heard it. The Cherokee version in which Cricket is a barber who helps Rabbit by clipping the hair off possum's tail is found in *BAEAR* 19:1, p. 269.

28. **Raven and Octopus Woman** is a story we have heard several times. This variant is retold from a version Teresa Pijoan of Algodones, New Mexico gave us in the summer of 1992. A more violent variant appears in *BAEAR* 31, p. 932.

29. **Ghost of the White Deer** Judy first heard at Star School, the two-room schoolhouse outside Wagoner, Oklahoma. The Dockrey family has lived in Oklahoma, in the Chickasaw and then the Cherokee Nation, from the late 1800s, through its statehood in 1907, up to the present.

30. **Dance of the Dead** we first heard in fragmentary form at Silver Dollar City in 1992, then found in *University of California Publications in American Archaeology and Ethnology*, Vol. 4 (1904) and Vol. 8 (1908).

31. **The Girl Who Married a Ghost** is a story we have heard since 1983, and our version is based on the Blue Jay stories found in K. B. Judson's *Myths and Legends of the Pacific Northwest* (Chicago: A. C. McClurg & Co., 1910) and from Blue Jay and Robin stories in *BAEB* 20, p. 167.

Glossary

Albino   An animal or human being born without skin coloring. Albinos have snow-white skin, white hair and colorless eyes that look red. (Your eyes might look red in a flash photograph, but an albino's eyes look red all the time.)

Animal People   Native Americans usually regarded animals as just another kind of people or tribe who could think and talk and act according to their own needs. In many stories animals are described with human characteristics such as hair tied in the manner of a particular tribe.

Blue corn   Maize, which we call corn, comes in several colors: blue, yellow, white, and red. The corn is actually the color named, and when it is cooked, the tortillas or bread come out that color.

Bois d'arc   Bow-wood, or wood from the Osage orange tree, from which good bows are made.

Cane screen   A wall made of lightweight river cane like bamboo, stuck in the ground to screen off an area or a doorway so that one can walk around it, but others cannot see past it.

Clan   A group of people who are related to each other, but are not immediate family; a gathering of families within a tribe.

Council   Each tribe has a governing body called a council, usually led by one or more chiefs. Some tribes have more than one council, sometimes a men's council and a women's council.

Cradle-board   A backpack for carrying babies with a lightweight wooden frame about two feet long. Mothers often carried their babies with them while they worked.

Doeskin   The skin of a female deer. The skin of a male deer is called buckskin.

Five Tribes   Originally called the Five "Civilized" Tribes, a name now considered insulting to other Indians. The tribes are the Cherokee, Chicasaw, Choctow, Seminole, and Muskogee (or "Creek").

Frybread   A flat pancake of bread or cornbread fried in a pan or on a hot rock.

Give away   A ceremony during which a proud, wealthy family gives gifts to friends and even strangers as a community service and to show off their wealth.

Gorget   A decorative piece of wide bone or shell on a necklace.

Great River   Each Indian tribe called the biggest river it knew of "the Great River." In "The Girl Who Married A Ghost," it refers to the Columbia River.

Great Waters   The ocean; in "How The Animals Got Their Colors," the Pacific Ocean off the coast of Washington and Oregon.

Head man   The man in charge of a work gang, a hunting party, a war party or a whole village; similar to a temporary chief.

Herbs   Plants or the leaves of plants that have medicinal value, or affect human behavior, or have special spiritual value.

Indian Hen   Another name for the pileated woodpecker.

Kicking-stick toy   A decorated wooden stick that is kicked around in a Pueblo game the way a soccer ball is kicked around.

Litter   A stretcher made of two poles and animal skin used to carry wounded or ill people from place to place.

Lodge   A large house made of logs or logs and earth; the home of one or more Indian families.

Long house The large bark lodge that several Indian families shared. They were often twenty feet tall, thirty feet wide and in New England, Eastern Canada, and the Northeast, sixty feet long.

Mace A stone war club used to strike enemies in battle, also a symbol of the chief's authority.

Meal beaters Tall stone bowls in which corn was beaten with tall wooden pounders carved from logs. A man or woman stood up to use a meal beater, so the pounder and bowl stood four feet high. The corn was beaten into meal, and the meal used to make cornbread.

Mesa A low, flat-topped hill or mountain in the desert Southwest.

Moon A period of 28 days, the Indians' word for "month."

People Human beings of a specific tribe. Although each tribe has a name that it calls itself (for example, the people we call *Navajo* call themselves *Dineh* instead) the name almost always translates into English as "The People." People are sometimes called "Human People" to distinguish them from Animal People.

Pitch The gummy sap of an evergreen tree, used as glue and varnish.

Powwow A gathering, an important meeting, a big dance with many people, or a healing ceremony.

Prayer sticks When some Native Americans pray, they lay out painted, decorated sticks. Different sticks are used for different kinds of prayer.

Race Indians loved foot races; the race course was always oval-shaped and started and ended at the same spot. There was usually a stick at the turn-around point.

Sachem Chief of a tribe in New England.

Shipap The hole in the earth that led Human People out from under the ground, where Pueblo People say we all began. This hole could lead from the spirit world to this world above or, as it did for Turkey Girl, from this world to the spirit world below.

Sinew   Dried tendon used as string. Tendons are the tough, white connective tissues that fasten muscle to bone; when dried, they are like leather and very strong.

Six Nations   Originally organized in 1451, the "Confederated Tribes" or Iroquois Confederation, consists of the Seneca, Mohawk, Oneida, Onondaga, Cayuga, and joining later, the Tuscarora.

Soaproot   The hard, greasy root of a cactus that foams like soap and cleans like soap when rubbed under water. Agave and aloe are examples of soaproot plants.

Trickster   A character or being in a story who plays tricks on others. Some tricksters are wise, others are foolish; some give great gifts and wisdom to human beings who ask for it.

War chant   Like a war song, but sung on only one or two musical notes.

War song   A song sung loudly to frighten your enemy and stir up your own faith and courage.

Water panther   An evil beast that lived in rivers and lakes in Indian stories about ancient times.

Other Books from
August House Publishers

White Wolf Woman
and Other Native American Transformation Myths

Teresa Pijoan explores the common spirit which binds together
all forms of life through more than 40 transformation myths.

Hardback $17.95 / ISBN 0-87483-201-2
Paperback $8.95 / ISBN 0-87483-200-4

American Indians'
Kitchen-Table Stories
Contemporary Conversations with Cherokee, Sioux, Hopi, Osage, Navajo, Zuni, and Members of Other Nations

Keith Cunningham collects more than 200 narratives
from conversations with contemporary Native American storytellers.

Hardback $25.95 / ISBN 0-87483-203-9
Paperback $14.95 / ISBN 0-87483-202-0

Rachel the Clever
and Other Jewish Folktales

Forty-six tales brought to America by immigrants from
countries and regions as diverse as the stories.
Collected and retold by Josepha Sherman.

Hardback $18.95 / ISBN 0-87483-306-X
Paperback $9.95 / ISBN 0-87483-307-8

African-American Folktales

Stories from the black oral tradition that transcend color and culture
collected and edited by Richard and Judy Dockrey Young.

Hardback $18.95 / ISBN 0-87483-308-6
Paperback $9.95 / ISBN 0-87483-309-4

August House Publishers
P.O. Box 3223, Little Rock, Arkansas 72203
1-800-284-8784